She could hear the sea in the background, could smell it in the air. But even with the reassuring, steady rhythm of waves hitting rocks, she still felt like the last person left on earth. Until her peripheral vision caught sight of a shadow looming through a pocket of mist.

The dogs sounded closer, too, one of them appearing at the shadow's feet. And then a voice called one of them, followed by a whistle. So Keelin knew the figure was male.

The mist swirled again. The sun came out and caught in a glint off his dark hair. And Keelin stood transfixed as he got closer and looked straight at her.

He was sensational.

Dear Reader,

Between my first and second book sales, I was fortunate enough to spend eight months touring every county of Ireland with an amazing group of people. For one idyllic week we stayed on Valentia Island, off the coast of County Kerry, and the place has stayed in my mind ever since—maybe just waiting for this story to come along.

Valentia is isolated, beautiful and inspiring. It has one tiny village at one end, where the ferry brings visitors from the mainland, and a single-lane bridge at the other end, for times when the ferry can't run in bad weather. Although it has a rich history all of its own, it is the sea that has had the most profound effect on the islanders. Over the years they have manned the lighthouses and the lifeboats, dealt with pirates and traders, Manx men and Spaniards, Cromwellian soldiers and pioneering aviators. And the marine life attracts people like me, who are fascinated by the sight of dolphins swimming within eyesight of the coast.

When you then add the coast of Kerry, its mountains and green fields framed by the crashing waves of the Atlantic below and the wide expanse of open sky above—a panoramic view from almost every angle of the island—you'll understand why it called out for a love story like Garrett and Keelin's.

So, if you ever visit Ireland and drive to County Kerry… take a little time. Visit Valentia Island and bide awhile. It'll be worth it—trust me. Troubled souls have found a little piece of heaven there.

Hugs and kisses,

Trish

TRISH WYLIE
Bride of the Emerald Isle

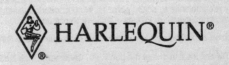

TORONTO • NEW YORK • LONDON
AMSTERDAM • PARIS • SYDNEY • HAMBURG
STOCKHOLM • ATHENS • TOKYO • MILAN • MADRID
PRAGUE • WARSAW • BUDAPEST • AUCKLAND

ISBN-13: 978-0-373-03964-7
ISBN-10: 0-373-03964-6

BRIDE OF THE EMERALD ISLE

First North American Publication 2007.

www.eHarlequin.com

Printed in U.S.A.

Trish Wylie tried various careers before eventually fulfilling her dream of writing. Years spent working in the music industry, in promotions and teaching little kids about ponies gave her plenty of opportunity to study life and the people around her—which, in Trish's opinion, is a pretty good study course for writing! Living in Ireland, Trish balances her time between writing and horses. If you get to spend your days doing things you love, then she thinks that's not doing too badly. You can contact Trish at www.trishwylie.com.

Trish says she's always believed that everything happens for a reason. And in this book her belief in that was echoed without her even thinking about it. Keelin, the heroine, not only finds what she was searching for, but she heals wounds of old for others along the way. All from one chance find amongst her mother's belongings. Writing this story left Trish with a smile on her face for days—if it does the same for others, then she'll be a happy girl.

For my brother Neil—whose birthday
I completely forgot while writing this book....

CHAPTER ONE

KEELIN O'DONNELL had always been a morning person. But today was testing her love of the a.m. to its limits...

She paused, looked back down the road, and sighed. The house had to be somewhere near by now, surely? Did people still die on the moors?

There was the sound of barking nearby.

'Great.' She scowled as she looked towards the source of the sound. 'Now I'm going to be eaten by wild dogs. The Hound of the Baskervilles lives.'

The barking sounded closer again. Not so much of a rabid-dog sound as an excited yapping, which made her feel vaguely better, so her blue eyes searched what she could see of the surrounding countryside. With the last of the early morning mist clearing she could finally see more than the outline of the old stone walls on either side of her. Now there were fields, swirling with a hint of mist in pockets where the ground was still wet with morning dew.

She could hear the sea in the background, could smell it in the air. But even with the reassuring, steady rhythm of waves hitting rocks, she still felt like the last person left on earth. Until her peripheral vision caught sight of a shadow looming through a pocket of mist.

The dogs sounded closer, too, one of them appearing at the shadow's feet. And then a voice called one of them, followed by a whistle. So Keelin knew the figure was male. A man walking straight towards her—practically dreamlike—like some kind of early morning ghost.

The mist swirled again in pockets at his feet, the sun came out and caught in a glint off his dark hair. And Keelin stood transfixed as he got closer and looked straight at her.

He was sensational.

Straight out of the pages of some big-city magazine trying to sell country-wear to women who dearly hoped those clothes would make their citified men turn into this Adonis.

But as his tall, lean frame made its way over the uneven ground, two bouncing Springer Spaniels at his heel, Keelin almost felt transported back in time.

It was the clothes. It had to be. Long, waxed coat, open necked loose shirt; he even had a walking stick, for crying out loud! If Heathcliff had looked half as good in the early morning light on the moors then it was a wonder Cathy ever let him go…

As he got closer, his gaze still fixed on her, Keelin felt her mouth go dry. Where had this kind of man been hiding away from the world? Here, on some tiny island off the coast of Co. Kerry? *What a waste.*

'Good morning.'

Lord, he even sounded good; the most gorgeously deep, multifaceted, rumbling masculine tone. *A symphony of a voice.* Was he real?

Keelin stared up at him as he got closer, blinking her eyes slowly in stark appreciation. After all, she'd always been a bit of a sucker for tall, dark and handsome. What woman wasn't?

Say something, Keelin!

She silently cleared her throat and managed a husky. 'Hello.'

Oh, great start.

The man continued staring at her. 'Are you lost?'

If his eyes were as great close up as the rest of him looked from a few feet away, then there was a very good chance she would be, but. 'Not according to the man in the hotel who gave me directions, no.'

'Patrick?' He smiled briefly, white teeth flashing and a momentary hint of deep dimples appearing on his cheeks as he continued closing the distance between them. 'Told you it was only a stretch of the legs, did he?'

With legs the length of this man's it probably was. But Keelin was only five feet five on a heels day. And Valentia Island was hardly the place for heels.

She nodded resignedly. 'A regular running joke for him, is it?'

'Afraid so.' His gaze still fixed on her, he reached one large hand down to a bouncing dog, which wagged its tail manically in appreciation. 'Where were you looking to get to?'

'Inishmore House.' Keelin tried her best not to feel jealous of a wet dog. After all, no one had patted her head since she was nine and she'd hated it then. 'It's s'posed to be out here somewhere. And I read in a brochure that this island was only seven miles across so I can't have too much further to go before I fall off the other side.'

'Oh, you've a mile or two to go before that happens.'

'That's reassuring.'

He made the final few steps to the opposite side of the stone wall, which created a barrier between them. Keelin was momentarily distracted as one set of paws appeared on top of it, rocking a loose stone. The dog looked up at her with a tilted head, pondering her with soulful brown eyes before its long tongue appeared and it appeared to grin at her.

Smiling softly in response, Keelin let her eyes stray upwards to meet his. Rich, toffee colored eyes, framed with thick dark lashes. And she had to make herself pat the smiling dog's damp head to keep herself from sighing loudly in contentment. She'd always been easily swayed by great eyes. And this man had sensational eyes. But being a connoisseur had always led her into heartache before.

And a man like this one didn't live in a tiny place like this alone, did he?

'What brings someone like you to Inishmore House?'

That was probably as close to *'What's a nice girl like you doing in a place like this?'* that Keelin had heard in a while.

Drop-dead gorgeous men who seemed to tug at every sense she possessed were a rare occurrence, so she didn't really know how she was supposed to deal with that. But corny one-liner chat-up lines she could deal with.

After all, she hadn't come all this way to look for a new love interest, had she? No matter how sensational he was to look at. It would be the kind of complication she really didn't need at this point in her life.

Nope, she had bigger things to deal with. She really couldn't allow herself to get so easily distracted.

So she drew on her wealth of social experience and changed her tone, became a little less warm, more businesslike. Making it clear she had somewhere to be, something important to do. 'I'm looking for someone, is it nearby?'

'A short stretch of the legs from here.'

Keelin stared up at him, unamused. 'That's very funny.'

There was a sudden deep chuckle of laughter. And the deep, resonating rumble touched her somewhere deep inside. Briefly. As lasting as a single heartbeat, but she felt it echo through her like the ripple in a pool. And for a following brief moment, it frightened the life out of her.

It was obviously something in the atmosphere. It had to be. The setting, the mist, the lengthy dramatic entrance he'd made across the field looking the way he did. She was being seduced by the moment. That was all.

A form of escapism from her fear of the thing she was here to discover, possibly?

She squared her shoulders. There wasn't any time for fantasy here. She hadn't travelled halfway across the country to fawn over the first good-looking man she met.

'If you could just point me in the right direction? That would be very helpful, thank you.'

'I can do better than that.' He set his walking stick on the wall and, leaning on one hand, vaulted over it, landing neatly on his feet in front of her as she stepped back to make room for him. He then studied her up close and personal, his toffee eyes meltingly warm.

'I'll take you there.'

Oh, no, Keelin didn't think so. She read a lot of murder mysteries, thank you. And this man was dangerous enough as it was, looking and sounding the way he did…

'No, it's fine, thanks. I can find it if you point me the right way.'

'I'm going that way.'

Not with her, he wasn't. 'Really, I'm sure I can—'

'Aren't there any gentlemen left in the big cities these days?'

Not so much. But that wasn't the point. 'You're a complete stranger, I don't know you.'

'Well, that's easily remedied.' He reached out a large hand. 'I'm Garrett—'

'I don't actually *need* to know who you are, either. I'm sorry. I just need to get where I'm going. I'm not here to get picked up by strangers in the middle of nowhere.'

The hand dropped back to his side. 'Bit full of yourself, aren't you?'

Keelin noted how his face remained impassive, but a twinkle of light stayed in his eyes, hinting at his amusement. Lord, but he was tempting. A nine point nine on the Romance Richter scale. But she refused point-blank to allow herself to be swayed by him. Her mother had come to this place once and been 'swayed' and look where that had got her!

The thought refocused her, so, instead of allowing herself to be tempted by his obvious charms, she frowned, crossing her arms across her chest and tilting her chin as she answered. 'Look, Mr—'

'Garrett.'

Her frown upgraded to a scowl at the sound of his steady deep tone and her own visceral response to it. Well, her attempt at a cool brush-off hadn't worked, so she'd have to be direct.

'*Garrett.* I'm sure there's more than enough female fodder amongst the usual tourists here to keep you amused for a few months a year. But I'm not a tourist. Neither am I on the market as fodder. And I won't be here long enough to be swayed by you turning on the rustic charm. So why don't you just point a finger in the general vicinity of where I need to go and I'll spread the word to the tourist board about how friendly the locals are.' She added a sugary-sweet smile for good measure.

'I thought you said you weren't a tourist?'

The calm tone to his voice made her falter briefly. 'I'm not.'

'Well, then, how are you going to tell the tourist board that you noticed I had rustic charm?'

What was she now, a magnet for wise guys? Perfect. She sighed. 'Forget it. I'll find it myself.'

Even that jolly local prankster Patrick wouldn't have sent her in the *wrong* direction.

Garrett fell into step beside her and when she glared sideways at him she almost tripped over one of the Springers.

One large hand shot out and caught her elbow, steadying her, long fingers curling in and around as she leaned briefly into his strength.

But she recovered quickly, snatching her elbow away, yanking her body back from his, and spinning round to look up at him while still glaring. 'Would you just *go away?*'

'I already told you I was going this way.'

'Well, then, I'll just wait right here 'til you're gone before I start walking again.'

His mouth quirked, teasing at his dimples as he silently watched her folding her arms again. Then he mirrored the movement, blinking down at her with an intense gaze. 'Are you always this rude to someone who's trying to be a gentleman?'

'Only when I'm stranded in the middle of what could be, as far as I know, the killing fields of Co. Kerry. Bodies might never be found way out here.'

'Do I look like a mass murderer to you?'

'You wouldn't have to be a mass murderer—there's only *one* of me.'

His eyes glowed. 'Well, I'm one of the good guys, honest. And *I* know where I'm going. You could dander on up this road and walk off the cliffs if I let you. And that would *definitely* ruin my reputation as a good guy.'

Keelin stared at him for a long, long moment. Well, just *because...*

Then she finally shook her head, recognizing that the spark in his eyes was teasing, not the least little bit threatening. Though how she could possibly have known that so surely after ten minutes stunned her. It was too surreal. She just really needed coffee—a nice mocha cappuccino maybe. And the gentle hum of traffic in the background that would fill the 'if you scream noone will hear you' void. And not to have walked so far already in one morning would be good, too.

Mind you, so would sleeping a single wink the night before she'd come out on this quest of hers in the first place...

When she said nothing, merely unfolding her arms and

staring up at him, Garrett's mouth twitched again. He was obviously easily amused.

One of the bouncing Springers seemed to notice there was tension in the air and decided to help dissipate it by jumping up to say hello, leaving a matching set of paw-prints on her pale beige trousers.

Keelin flinched, as much out of surprise as anything else. She liked dogs, *normally.*

'Down, Ben!' Garrett's voice sounded firmly and the dog obeyed immediately, moving around his master's legs to sit at his side before looking upwards with an expression of apologetic adoration.

Keelin glanced down at her trousers. 'Oh, terrific.' She raised both arms from her sides and let them drop. 'That's just great.'

'They're a little over-friendly at times.'

Ignoring the rueful tone to his voice she smiled sarcastically. 'Seems to be a glut of that here, doesn't there?'

His eyes studied the paw-prints, then dropped lower. 'Are those supposed to be wellingtons?'

Keelin looked down too. 'They *are* wellingtons.'

She should know; she'd bought them especially for her trip, after all. Not much call for wellingtons in the middle of Dublin.

When he continued to study them she raised her eyes and studied the top of his head. Lord, he even had gorgeous hair: thick, sleek, deep chocolate brown, the kind of hair that begged to have fingers thread through it.

What were they talking about again? *Oh, yes.* 'What's wrong with them?'

'They have flowers on them.'

Keelin nodded and spoke slowly. 'Y-e-s, *I'm* a *girl.*'

His head rose, toffee eyes sparkling again as his voice dropped to a more intimate tone. 'Yeah, I got that.'

Her cheeks warmed.

'It's just that wellingtons normally come in green or black.'

'Or *navy?*' She batted her eyelashes.

Garrett nodded slowly. 'Sometimes in navy.'

There was a brief silence. While Keelin stared into his eyes and momentarily forgot how to think. She could feel her pulse beating erratically, could hear her heart thudding against the wall of her chest. *Aw, c'mon!* She was getting turned on by a conversation about wellington boots now? How sad did that make her?

'You really need to get off this island more, you know that, right?'

'Explore the world of possibilities available to wellington wearers worldwide?'

'Exactly. Broaden your horizons some.'

He stepped a little closer, lowering his head to grumble. 'You see, I would, but *I'm* a *boy*. We happen to *like* green, black or navy. It's much more practical.'

Keelin swallowed convulsively.

'So—' he smiled a slow, sensual smile '—you ready to walk a little more? Now that we know where we stand on the wellingtons issue?'

'You're not going to let me walk on my own, are you?' She somehow knew that instinctively.

Garrett shook his head. 'Nope.'

Damnable chivalry! Whose idea was *that* in the modern era? Women like Keelin really weren't used to being treated this way!

Allowing herself just a second more of up-close study, she then forced herself to look away, sighing dramatically. 'Well, lead on, then, if you must. But if we get near anything that remotely resembles a shallow grave, I warn you—I've taken classes in self-defence.'

There was another low, rumbled chuckle of laughter beside her as they fell into step along the narrow laneway. 'You've been in the city too long.'

'What makes you so sure I'm *from* the city?'

'It's written all over you. You look—' his face turned to study her profile '—expensive.'

Keelin tilted her head his way as she walked. 'Now, Garrett, did you just go calling me high maintenance?'

His mouth quirked yet again. 'Are you telling me you're not?'

If only he knew. 'If you knew me better you'd know I'm one of the least high-maintenance women on the planet. But, please, feel free to jump to conclusions.'

'That's why you're enjoying being on the island so much already, I take it?'

No, that wasn't why she wasn't enjoying the island.

She focused her gaze forwards, following the gentle sweep of the narrow stone-wall-lined laneway she was walking along, to where it had branched out in two different directions. It could almost have been metaphor, but then every path taken had a set of choices, right? She sighed, and a confession rolled off her reluctant tongue.

'It's not the island's fault. I just get a little tense when I'm nervous.'

'And I'm making you nervous, am I?'

She glanced his way again with a small, mischievous smile. '*Now* who's full of themself?'

He smiled a glorious, full, dimpled smile in return and Keelin found herself laughing.

Garrett leaned his head a little closer. 'That's better. See, *now* you look less high maintenance.'

She was still smiling in amusement as his focus went back to his dogs, his upper lip flattening briefly against straight white teeth as he whistled them back into closer proximity.

'Do you flirt with every woman who gets lost on this island, then?'

When he glanced at her, his warm eyes were so intense she almost caught her breath. 'Maybe you just bring that out in me.'

Keelin rolled her eyes, which was rewarded with another low chuckle of laughter.

Both looking up the laneway, they fell into an almost companionable silence for a while before his voice sounded again. 'So why are you nervous?'

Ah, now there was a question. 'Let's just say I'm still not entirely sure what I'm doing here.'

'You know someone at Inishmore?'

'No. Not yet.'

They walked another couple of steps. 'Is someone expecting you?'

'I'd think it's safe to say no one is, no.'

Out of her peripheral vision she saw him nod, as if he was confirming something he already knew. 'So, are you the bearer of bad news, then?'

Even though she knew he was just seeking a logical explanation for her nervousness, Keelin faltered. Tilting her head back slightly, she looked up at the rapidly clearing blue skies above her, her voice low. 'Sort of.'

Garrett leaned forwards and looked down at her upturned face. And he smiled an encouraging smile when she looked at him. 'No one likes to be the bearer of bad news. It's no wonder you're nervous.'

Keelin stared, transfixed as he smiled down at her. Then his hand reached up again, cupping her elbow briefly, squeezing in reassurance. 'They're not bad people. They won't shoot the messenger.'

'That really depends on what the messenger tells them, doesn't it?'

A dark brow quirked. 'Is it the messenger's fault?'

'No.' The whispered word came out on a small sigh as a

wave of emotion swept over her. She really had thought she was better prepared for this. But she was out on a limb further than she'd ever been. And it was terrifying. When she had told him she still wasn't sure what she was doing here, it hadn't been entirely a lie. Not entirely.

She had reasoned with herself that she could handle it if she was turned away. If she was rejected. But there was still a part of her that would hurt deeply if she was. If she didn't find out what it was she was looking for.

It would be pain on top of anguish and grief that she was barely holding together as it was. Maybe she should just have let it be. Left the past in the past and got on with building her future, instead of standing beside a complete stranger with a confession on the tip of her tongue.

The large hand on her elbow exerted a little pressure, bringing her out of her sorrowful reverie, so that she was forced to look up again.

Garrett smiled a slow, soft smile and the depth of warmth that emanated from it brought an equal warmth to her chest in reply that was surprisingly soothing.

She stared at him with wide, curious eyes. She'd just never met a man quite like him before. And she couldn't even put it down to the romance of rolling mists and a grand entrance into her line of vision. There was just *something* about him, something that held her attention, fascinated her more than she'd ever been fascinated before.

He was *compelling*. Yes. Compelling was a good word.

Toffee eyes roamed over her face and his hand dropped from her arm. 'Dermot Kincaid is a good man. He'll listen to what you have to say, whatever it might be.'

Keelin's eyes widened. 'You know him?'

Garrett's eyes sparkled briefly again as they began walking once more. 'Yes, it's safe to say I know him as well as anyone.

And judging by the look on your face a minute ago, whatever you've come to see him for is important. He'll see that too, if you'll give him a chance. Not all us island folk are potential mass murderers…'

She found it difficult to breathe, her chest suddenly tight. So that it took a few moments before she could find a single question to ask from the long list she'd been forming on her way to the island. 'What's he like?'

Garrett's eyes took on a far-off expression before he looked away from her face. 'Like any other man his age. Has lived and learned some, so sometimes has entirely too much common sense, which can be annoying if you're convinced you're in the right when he knows you're not. And he's formed some strong opinions along the way, so can be a real stubborn-headed goat when he wants to be.' He grinned briefly at her, dimples flashing.

'But he still has an appreciation for a good-looking girl, so you'll be just fine.'

Keelin felt her cheeks warm again.

And Garrett caught sight of it before he laughed. 'Yeah, he'll like you all right, even if he is old enough to be your father.'

She was glad he turned his face away as he threw out the latter.

'That's the house over there.'

The hand that had been subconsciously straightening the material over the elbow he had held onto froze as her gaze followed his pointing finger to the large, old stone farmhouse ahead of them.

Garrett stopped a few steps in front of her and turned, a quizzical expression on his face when she remained still. 'What's wrong?'

Keelin frowned. She had been so momentarily transfixed by the sight of her destination that she had forgotten he was there. And she wasn't about to explain to him why it was suddenly so difficult to take the final steps to get there. How could he possibly understand that, to her, it had taken a lifetime to reach this place?

So she sought a safer answer. 'And you couldn't have just told me it was round the next bend?'

He smiled laconically. 'And ruin all the fun?'

Hitching her chin up a very visible inch, Keelin walked past him with determined steps in flowered wellingtons. 'You *really* need to get off this island more.'

It didn't occur to her addled mind that he was still following along with her until his dogs stopped at the small gateway, wagging their tails as they waited for it to be opened. Keelin stopped, looked down at them, and then up at Garrett's face as he reached for the latch.

'You don't need to see me to the door. I can take it from here.'

'I already told you I was going this way.'

'I didn't think you meant all the way *into* the house.'

With his hand holding the gate open, dogs already having galloped ahead, Garrett leaned his head a little closer, and smiled another heart-stopping smile. 'I have to go in. I live here.'

Keelin's eyes widened to the size of saucers. 'You *live here?*'

Garrett nodded very slowly. 'Yes, I live here, for the moment anyway. I'm building a house nearby, but this has been home for a long time. I did try introducing myself but you were having none of it. And incidentally—' a single eyebrow quirked at her '—I didn't catch *your* name….'

Still reeling with the new information, Keelin had to struggle to keep up. 'Maybe because I didn't give it. And you didn't ask.'

'Well—' he leaned back and took a breath '—that we can fix.'

She watched as he reached a large hand out towards her, but hesitated accepting it, in making the simple skin-to-skin contact involved with setting her smaller hand into his.

And he quirked a single eyebrow again in question.

So, with a deep breath, and a brief run of the end of her

her contradiction. City women were way too self-
to blush, weren't they? They were in Garrett's ex-
. He'd found that kind of confidence sexy *once*, that

nce had been enough.

knowing that, you'd think he'd have had the sense to
to himself, wouldn't you?' Dermot waved a hand in
direction. 'Get the girl a cup of tea, then. The pot's
on top of the stove.'

tt merely lifted an eyebrow in question as she looked
And she smiled a very small smile in response. So he
'Milk, no sugar, I suppose?'

girl's second preference to some foreign froth of a
his experience...

k you.'

own, sit down.' Dermot pulled out a chair for her at the
ell-worn kitchen table. 'Keelin, is it? What a lovely
re you here for a bit of a holiday? Do you know the
all? It's a lovely place, isn't it?'

might be able to answer if you paused for breath.'
hrew the words over his shoulder as he reached for a
poured steaming tea into it. 'Let her get a word in.'

nat he doubted her ability to do that if she chose. But
g had changed when she'd walked through the door
rett was keen to have his father let her get to it.

uriosity was killing *him*.

not here on holiday.'

rrett turned to place the mug in front of her she was
long strap of her bag from across her shoulders, shrug-
head below it before she searched through its contents
ere to bring you something I think belongs to you.'

e?' Dermot's eyes widened in surprise. 'Are you sure
t?'

tongue over her dry lips, she placed her hand in his. And felt the immediate sliver of warmth run through her fingers and up her arm. 'I'm Keelin O'Donnell.'

'Hello, Keelin O'Donnell.' Still holding her hand in his, he inclined his head slightly. 'It's nice to meet you. I'm Garrett Kincaid.'

'Kincaid?'

Again in that deeply hypnotic tone. 'Yes, Kincaid.'

Keelin let go of his hand as if he'd burned her, rubbing her palm up and down against her thigh as she stared up at him.

Garrett in turn held his now-free hand out to the side, beckoning her through the gateway. 'My father will be in the kitchen.'

Keelin walked through the gateway on automatic pilot. *His father.* His father, whom she had come all this way to find. It held a certain irony that she would feel something in the wrong place at the wrong time, would meet the first man in a long time whom she found compelling, too attractive for his own good, who had made the most perfect of perfect entrances into her already complicated life. And then discover that, rather than being a mass murderer, this gorgeously compelling male could, in all likelihood, already be out of bounds...as a potential family member...

Or, Lord help her, he could even be a brother!

CHAPTER TWO

As THE dogs scampered across the tiled floor to their baskets Garrett watched the sylph-like blonde hovering in the doorway, a look of sheer terror on her face.

She was quite the mystery woman, wasn't she?

And, to be honest, he'd thought that before he had even found out where she was going. It wasn't too often he bumped into a beautiful woman in the middle of nowhere first thing in the morning…

Especially not one he'd felt drawn to the way he had to her. There was just, *something,* about her. What was it?

'You checked the herd?' His father's voice sounded out from in front of the huge range that dominated the kitchen, his back to the door. 'All still in one piece?'

'Yes, all present and accounted for.' He jerked his head. 'Come on in, Keelin.'

She took a deep breath and walked into the room, her eyes immediately seeking out its only other occupant.

Who in turn turned to face her with curious eyes. 'Where on earth did you find this lovely creature? I've been sending you out to check stock for decades and you never came home with one of these.'

'She's not here to see me. She's here to see you.'

A mischievous light entered Dermo_ at Keelin before walking over and sla_ back. 'Son, really, you shouldn't have. It next month.'

But the attempt at humour washed r_ seemed to be growing paler by the second ethereal look, with her already pale skin _ blue eyes. And in the second it took for hand in greeting she seemed to shrink a l_ ing almost glasslike, as if his touch mig_

And Garrett *really* wanted to know _ contradictions—sassy city girl one minu_ nocently childlike the next. Who _ O'Donnell?

He cleared his throat. 'Paddy McIlroy the hotel in Knightstown.'

'*On foot?*' Dermot looked over at hi_ Keelin finally shook his hand. 'Good st_

Keelin seemed to recover as she took think he used the word "good" or "fair". known to use my car.'

'He has a very individual sense of h_ 'Yes, I got that.'

'So what brings you up to visit us, t_ of a lovely girl doesn't brighten any day

Garrett couldn't hold back a smile _ his head closer to Keelin's as he peeled you'd like you.'

Colour returned to Keelin's face as a_ way onto her cheeks. And, despite his_ smiled all the more. He liked the fact th_ A rare thing in the modern age. Especi_ lived in the big city.

'Yes.' Her eyes flickered briefly to his face, then up to Garrett's as he set down the mug. 'Thank you.'

Garrett smiled encouragingly. 'You already said thank you. It's only a cup of tea, Keelin O'Donnell, it's not that big a deal.'

There was a sudden silence. Broken by. *'O'Donnell?'*

Garrett's gaze narrowed as his father repeated her surname in the same surprised tone Keelin had when he'd said his name was Kincaid at the gate. What the hell was going on?

Keelin faltered, her hand rising from the bag with a bundle of faded blue letters that she laid on the table in front of her, both hands then smoothing over them as she studied his father's face.

'Yes.'

The answer was low, almost flat, yet determined. And the reaction on Dermot's face was dramatic. He stared at her long and hard, as if he was searching for something, lost for words for the first time that Garrett could ever remember. Which was saying something.

And when Garrett looked back at Keelin, she was studying Dermot in exactly the same way.

Then her eyes flickered back up to meet his and Garrett felt a wave cramp the region of his chest. She looked lost. And he suddenly remembered what he had said to her about his father listening to whatever she had to say. How he had reassured her it would be all right.

Garrett was no liar. And he wouldn't let his old man make one of him either.

So he pinned a bright smile on his face and pulled out the chair beside her. 'So I take it you two know each other, then?'

He looked back and forth from one to the other.

Finally Dermot's eyes strayed to the letters that Keelin was stroking, colour fading from his face as he looked back up at her. 'Recently?'

The word was almost choked.

Keelin swallowed hard, her eyes shimmering as she nodded. 'Six weeks ago.'

'I'm sorry, child.'

She nodded again, her gaze dropping to her hands as she took a moment to control herself before she pushed the letters towards him. 'I thought you might want these.'

This time Dermot nodded. And even though Garrett now had a million and one questions, he didn't ask. It felt as if he would be intruding somehow—maybe already was simply by being there.

He watched as his father's fingers closed around the letters, drawing them closer to him on the table top before he smoothed his hands over them in the same way Keelin had. As if they were something very precious; something beyond any monetary value.

'Thank you, for bringing them.' His eyes rose to look at her face again, a small smile playing at the edges of his mouth as he spoke in a husky tone. 'You look like her.'

'I know.' Keelin smiled tremulously in return. 'I get told that all the time.'

'Aye, well you do. She was your age—' He stopped and cleared his throat. 'Garrett, get Keelin something to eat, would you? I'm sure she's hungry after that long walk.'

'I'm fine, really.' She flashed a small smile his way. 'I ate very early at the hotel.'

Garrett nodded. He couldn't seem to think of anything to say in the sight of her sparkling eyes and small smile. Damn but she was beautiful, really, an absolute stunner. What looking at her did to him took him back in time, reminded him of who he'd been a lifetime ago. And whoever it was she looked like must have had equally big an impression on his father.

Because the next thing he knew Dermot was pushing his chair back from the table, his fingers closing around the letters. 'You'll have to excuse me for a minute.'

Garrett watched in stark amazement as he left the room. *What—?*

There was the sound of chair legs scraping over the floor again as Keelin stood up and Garrett's gaze immediately returned to her face as she gathered her bag to her and spoke in a low voice. 'This was a mistake.'

'Wait.' His hand caught her smaller one on top of the bag, fingers curling round hers as he stood up. 'I'm sure he'll come back. This isn't like him.'

But then he wouldn't be the first Kincaid male to act strangely around this woman, would he?

Keelin untwisted her fingers from his and stepped back, her eyes avoiding his. 'No, really. I shouldn't have come here. I think I maybe knew that before I came.'

He could hear the tremor in her voice, could see the shimmer in her eyes as she glanced towards the door. And without thinking he knew he didn't want her to leave, not when she was so obviously upset.

Her being so upset was partly his fault, after all. He was the one who had told her his father wouldn't blame the messenger for whatever news she brought. Even though he still didn't really know what that news was.

'Who was he talking about?'

She swallowed again, frowning hard as she looked down at her flowered wellingtons. 'My mother.'

Six weeks ago.

Garrett put some of it together. 'She passed away?'

A single nod. 'Breast cancer.'

He flinched inwardly, floundering as he searched for something to say to her, annoyed with himself that he couldn't. He of all people should have been able to find some words. After all, she wouldn't be the first one he'd had to find the right words for when a mother had gone.

But while he frowned at the sudden flash of regret from his own past she turned, and was out of the door before he even had time to react.

When he did, without thought, he was immediately on her heels. 'Wait!'

Her hand was on the gate when he caught up with her, his hand on her shoulder, forcing her round to look at him. And when she did she wasn't able to hide the tears that streamed down her face.

Garrett swore.

She turned away again, fighting with the latch on the gate. 'I have to get out of here.' She shook the gate again as her voice cracked. 'What sort of a damn stupid gate *is this,* for crying out loud?'

He watched her struggling, a battle waging inside him between what propriety dictated he should do and what she might need most in that moment.

When her breath caught on a sob, he frowned hard, decision made. 'Leave it, Keelin. *Stop.*' He took a deep breath and stepped towards her. 'Come here.'

And even though it was entirely inappropriate with someone he had barely met, he drew her into his arms. 'I can't let you go running off in this state.'

She struggled in his arms. 'It's not your problem.'

'Maybe not, but if you run in the wrong direction and fall off the island, then I'll feel responsible.'

She struggled again. 'Let me go Garrett.'

'No. Just give yourself a minute.'

When she continued struggling, he spread his feet wider to support them both, even though she was so small in his arms. Then he waited, his arms firm around her waist until she went still, and sobbed against his chest, directly above his heart, so that the sound vibrated through him.

After a moment she seemed to soften, and Garrett felt his

shoulders relax, knowing she wasn't going to fight with him any more. So he waited again, his arms moving so that he could smooth his hands over her back as if he were soothing a wounded animal, trying to gain trust.

Her voice was muffled but stronger when she spoke. 'Well, this is a first.'

'Crying?' He tilted his chin down to study the top of her head as he attempted to inject a little humour. 'Don't all women do that?'

'No.' She lifted her head back a little so that her voice was clearer. 'I mastered that one the first time I saw a Lassie film. I've just never bawled all over someone within twenty minutes of meeting them.'

'You lost your mother. You have every right to cry. I just happen to be here, that's all.'

She stiffened in his arms again, then drew back, stepping away from him as she swiped at her cheeks with her palms. 'I really shouldn't have come here, I almost didn't make the trip. And now I know I shouldn't have. This was a *bad* idea.'

Garrett watched as she shook her head, his arms suddenly feeling redundant at his sides. So he shoved his hands into his pockets. 'I take it Dermot knew her?'

'A long time ago.'

'Well, he obviously never forgot her.'

Keelin flashed a brief smile his way. 'My mother had that effect on people. Once met, never forgotten.'

'Then I guess he was right when he said you were like her.'

Blue eyes widened as she shot him another glance, then she frowned and looked away. 'I better get back to the hotel.'

'I'll drive you back.'

'That's not necessary.'

'You already know how much of a stretch of the legs it is to get back there. Don't be daft.'

'The walk will do me good.'

'Tough.'

She was still frowning when she looked back at him, the city-girl confident façade back in place. 'Are you always this bossy?'

'Yep.' He flashed a half-smile at her. 'You'll get used to it. Most people do, given time.'

'I won't be here long enough to get used to it.'

'Well, then, consider this a one-shot deal.'

While she opened her mouth to answer that he took his hands out of his pockets and pointed a long finger at her. '*Don't move* and I'll go get my keys.'

'I can *walk*.'

'You could *try*. But I'll catch up with you in about a minute flat. So you may just think of this as a way of getting rid of me sooner. Otherwise I'm going to wind down the window and annoy you the whole way back. And I'm better at annoying than I am at bossy.'

By the time he had her seated in the passenger seat of his Range Rover, still scowling at him, Dermot had reappeared.

He tapped on Keelin's window, and Garrett hit the switch to wind it down.

'It took me a minute to find them. I'm sorry to have kept you waiting.'

Another bunch of letters was handed through the window and Keelin looked down at them as she took them from his hands, her face then rising, brows lifting in question.

Dermot smiled sadly. 'Call me sentimental if you like, but I kept hers, too. You should have them. So you can see both sides of the story.'

Keelin's voice was a low whisper. 'Thank you.'

A hand came through the window and squeezed her shoulder. 'Come back for dinner later. Garrett will come down and get you. I'd like to get a chance to know Breige's daughter, if that's all right with you?'

Garrett didn't realize he was holding his breath until she nodded. Then he smiled inwardly as he started up the engine and turned out onto the laneway.

'Told you he'd be back. Now you'll have a chance to get used to me being bossy.'

'I doubt one meal will do it.'

'Well, then, maybe I'll have to get Dermot to ask you to stay longer. You like him better than me.'

She rewarded him with a small, mischievous smile. 'He's better looking than you.'

Garrett shook his head as he looked out the windscreen. 'Nah, he's not.'

When she didn't argue his smile made it onto his face as he gave into a sudden pleasure that her mood had brightened. What man was ever comfortable with a crying woman, after all?

As they got closer to Knightstown he glanced across at her, where she held the bundle of letters hugged against her lap.

Garrett wanted to know the story behind those letters.

And not just because of the mystery that surrounded her mother and his father.

He needed to know why it was that a second generation of Kincaids was suddenly so fascinated by a second generation of O'Donnells.

Even though the second generation of Kincaids had no business being fascinated by a woman who came from the city. A woman who had no place on an island like Valentia. The two were like oil and water, Garrett knew. Because he'd already been badly burned once before.

So, the way he saw it, once his fascination waned with a little taste of familiarity, he could let it go. He wasn't about to be burned twice. No matter how beautiful Keelin O'Donnell was, or how drawn he'd been to hold her and offer her comfort.

No. He wouldn't put himself through it again. Casual and uninvolved worked much better for him these days if he felt the need for a female on his arm. And even if he was stupid enough to be tempted by anything more, he had responsibility for more than his own welfare now. He had Terri's to consider, too. And she was more important to him than anything else ever could be again.

Fascination, or no fascination.

CHAPTER THREE

KEELIN considered packing her bags and getting on the next ferry. But there was still a part of her that wanted to stay, to *know*, one way or the other. So she could put it behind her, close off another chapter before she moved on with her life.

She just hadn't factored a Garrett into the equation.

He had to be, what, early thirties? Which meant Dermot Kincaid had to have been a married man when her mother had met him. And, despite her mother's bohemian approach to life, that just didn't sit well on Keelin's shoulders.

Any more than being so attracted at first sight to someone who might be her half-brother did...

But then she had no way of knowing for sure that Dermot Kincaid was her father. Except that the dates were close enough to match. Well, at least that she could tell from his letters.

Her mother's letters might tell a different story.

But even as she sat on a bench overlooking Valentia Harbour, the vast panorama of the lush green countryside laid out before her like a painting her mother might have created early in her career, she couldn't bring herself to reach into her bag for them.

To have a direct line into a part of her mother's life that she hadn't known about.

It was just too glaring a reminder of how lacking their relationship had been while her mother was alive. Of what Keelin had missed out on by carrying around a sense of something major missing from her life, due to her mother's lifestyle and 'artistic' temperament.

Keelin had been so angry at her growing up. But even though they had made their peace before she'd left, Keelin was left with a hole inside, a hole she had hoped to fill with the things she had never known. As if somehow that could make it easier to move on…

This journey had been her attempt at trying to put the pieces together. To try and make sense of everything that had gone before so she could put it aside and move forwards. So she didn't feel as if she was drifting through life, filling in time, waiting for something she hadn't put a name to. While not really living at all.

'You're more like your father than me,' her mother would say to try and justify the glaring differences in their personalities when Keelin had been a rebellious teenager, determined her mother's way of living had ruined her own life in some way.

'How would I know that when you never talk about him?' had been Keelin's defence mid-argument.

She reached into her bag and took out the bundle of letters. They were her only chance to try and understand the woman who had never understood her, not really. And to try and put together the missing part of the puzzle that had led to her own existence.

She promised herself it didn't matter what Garrett thought about how she looked that evening. Even though she had taken an inordinate amount of time getting ready.

Living up to the memory Dermot had of her stunning mother would be difficult enough.

But the glow in Garrett's dark sable eyes when he turned to look at her in the tiny hotel foyer still brought a rush of welcomed self-confidence.

He didn't make a comment, though. Just slowly looked her down and back up.

And in that second she sent up a silent prayer that she could manage to control how attractive she found him, how he could have such an effect on her with just a glance. He took her breath away. He really did.

'I have to make a stop along the way.'

'No problem.' She pinned a bright smile in place as he eased his long legs in through the driver's side door.

'Just get ready for about a hundred questions.'

A rueful smile caused his dimples to flash briefly her way as he turned out onto the narrow street, executing a U-turn at the harbour. 'Terri is going to find you fascinating as all hell.'

Meaning he didn't? Not that it wouldn't be better if he didn't, but, surely, having been on the sidelines earlier, he couldn't help but at least be curious?

As she was now about the mysterious Terry. 'He doesn't get off the island much more than you do I take it?'

'She. And, no, she doesn't. No matter how much she bugs me on a daily basis about it.'

Not Terry, then. Theresa.

Keelin was suddenly ragingly curious about the kind of woman that Garrett spent time with. She was probably some excruciatingly pretty island girl who loved the outdoors and had wellingtons in one of the prerequisite colours. At least if she was interested in city life Keelin would have something to talk to her about.

Keelin the outsider might find a way not to feel so awkward in the company of two enigmatic Kincaid men that way. And with a girlfriend in tow then she could concentrate on trying to view Garrett as a friendly brother-figure rather than anything even resembling gorgeous male.

'You should take her for a nice romantic getaway in the city. She'd like that.'

Garrett laughed a low laugh beside her. 'Somehow I don't think dragging her old dad along on the trip would be part of the plan.'

Keelin gaped at his profile. 'You have a daughter?'

'Yes, that I most definitely do.'

'What age is she?'

'Fourteen.'

She gaped even more. He was obviously ageing better than she'd given him credit for.

When she didn't say anything, he glanced across at her, chuckling at her expression. 'Why do you look so surprised?'

Maybe because she was. 'You just don't look old enough to have a fourteen-year-old.'

'Careful now, that's almost a compliment.'

'What age *are* you?'

'Why is it women are always so quick to ask that question and never that keen on having it asked?'

'Twenty-seven in two months' time.' She smiled sugary-sweet when he glanced her way again. 'See, I have no problems with my age.'

'That's because you're only twenty-seven.'

'Still twenty-six, thank you.'

He chuckled again. 'Yep, no hang-ups about age there at all.'

She lifted her chin when he glanced across after turning onto a narrow lane. 'Spoken by the man who still hasn't fessed up to his. Having a fourteen-year-old ages you, you see.'

'More than you'll ever know.'

They made a right-handed turn and he slowed down to get through a set of gates. While Keelin smiled wistfully at his confession. She couldn't imagine what it would be like to have a teenager. Or a child, for that matter.

Even though for a while she had ached for one, so that she could do a better job with it than her mother had with her. But having a child involved a father in Keelin's mind. One that was there to watch his child grow.

And Keelin had never cared about any man enough for that to happen. To commit herself to a lifetime in his company. Which was the way she still believed it should be. Maybe that made her old-fashioned. But having grown up without one, with only the odd 'uncle' as a stand-in...

And Keelin didn't believe she should even start to look for a suitable candidate until she had sorted out her own life. It would hardly be fair on him, would it? No one should rely on someone else to sort out their problems, to take on their responsibilities for them. Not in this day and age. No, she would walk into a relationship a whole person or not at all. That way she would have equal footing with the man who would be a father to her children.

It took two people to make a marriage work.

They pulled up in front of a two-storey red-brick house and Garrett sounded the horn as he swung the Range Rover around.

'I was twenty when she was born.'

Keelin looked at him in surprise, *again*. Her mind immediately thinking back to the person she had been at twenty. She'd had enough of a problem dealing with herself without the added responsibility of a baby.

His eyes flickered briefly over her face again as the front door of the house opened. 'I'll let you do the maths.'

But, even while she worked it out, Keelin was already looking out of the side window to catch a glimpse of his daughter. She was the walking female version of her father. No denying *her* parentage. And she was tall, even for her age. Not quite as tall as her father, but certainly taller than Keelin. Not that that was difficult.

Though she had felt a little better in the hotel foyer, that, wearing heels, she at least made it to Garrett's shoulder. He just had a way of making her feel small and feminine that went way beyond her height and build.

'You're late, Dad.'

'No, I'm not. I just decided to get Keelin first so I could warn her about you.'

'Ha, ha.' She leaned between the seats and smiled at Keelin, her warm brown eyes lit with interest. 'Wow, you're beautiful! I love your hair. I'd like to go blonde.'

'You already think blonde.'

Keelin raised an arched brow at him and he grinned. 'No offence meant.'

'Well, I could take offence at that very easily.' She swallowed a smile as she tried to appear offended. But his grin teased it out of her and, instead, she shook her head at him in mock chagrin. 'Oh, don't listen to what *he* says. I never do.'

Keelin laughed aloud as Terri sat back and buckled her seat belt. And Garrett gave her a sparkling-eyed look that told her his daughter spoke the truth.

'I heard that Gramps knew your mum. They wrote letters to each other and everything. That's so romantic.'

Garrett's deep voice grumbled at Keelin's side. 'See? She does listen sometimes. Mostly when it's none of her business…'

'Like I wasn't going to listen in on this one. This is the most interesting thing to happen since Sean Leary's cow fell off the cliffs last winter.'

'You're kidding!' Keelin turned round in her seat, staring at Terri with wide eyes full of disbelief and amusement. 'It actually fell off the cliff?'

'Told you I had to be responsible about where you went this morning.'

She glanced briefly at Garrett from the corner of her eye before her attention was brought back to Terri, who waved a hand in front of her body.

'We had a stinker of a blizzard and the stupid thing forgot where it was. Sean said it looked like a fly on the windshield of a car.'

Garrett sighed. 'Sean didn't even see it. His father found it.'

'Well, his dad said it was well squished.'

'I'd imagine it would be.' Keelin felt a constant smile tugging at the corner of her mouth. 'I may not know much about cows, but I'm pretty sure they don't have wings.'

Terri grinned. 'Make them easier to milk if they could float over your head.'

Keelin laughed.

'Where are you from, then?'

Garrett's voice grumbled beside her again. 'She'll have you fill in a questionnaire before the end of the night.'

'Well, it's not like you were heavy on the details. I asked what you were like and he wouldn't tell me anything.' She rolled her eyes dramatically. *'Men!'*

'Well, you can see me for yourself now.'

'And you'd have thought he'd have mentioned how beautiful you are. It's not like my dad hangs round that many good-looking women.'

'That's right, ruin my reputation as a lady's man, why don't you?'

Keelin couldn't help but join in with the easy banter, feeling tension roll out of her for the first time in weeks. 'I thought you said you were a good guy?'

'Oh—' he stopped at the end of a road and looked directly into her eyes with a look that curled her toes '—I'm good all right.'

Keelin's eyes widened in shock at the innuendo, said as it was with that low rumbling tone of his. Wasn't he still a married man? What kind of married man flirted with another woman under his teenage daughter's gaze? She glanced at Terri to see if she'd heard, but Terri was looking out of the side window, her forehead creased into a frown as she thought.

But even so. It was bad form. And having had such a good impression of him so far, Keelin was disappointed, so she looked back at him and narrowed her eyes in warning.

His face stayed completely straight, as if he'd not meant anything by it at all. Mr Innocent.

Having had a moment to think, Terri looked back at her. 'So, where *are* you from?'

'Dublin, at the moment.'

'Cool! I'm gonna live in Dublin when I finish school.'

'Maybe.'

Terri scowled at the back of her father's head. 'Yes, *I am.* I've always wanted to live in the city.' She leaned forwards again. 'This place is *so* boring.'

Keelin could understand that to a teenage girl who had always lived there it would probably seem that way. She might even have felt the same way herself if the situations had been reversed. But to her, having a stable family life growing up, in somewhere as close knit as Valentia so obviously was, would have been heaven.

'But it'll be nice for you to have a home to come back to. I spent my whole childhood moving from one place to the next when all I really wanted was somewhere to call home.'

Had she just said that out loud?

She felt, rather than saw Garrett turning her way again, inwardly cringing at the bitter twist that might have come through in her voice.

But it wasn't just the man who had caught it.

'Didn't you have a home?'

She focused all her attention on Terri, who was the safer option in her mind. 'Oh, I had a home, lots of them, all over the place. Wherever we were my mother was always careful to give the appearance of it being a home.'

'Where'd you go?'

'London, New York, Paris, Rome, all the major cities at one time or another. Wherever my mother needed to be to promote her work or find her "muse".'

'Wow.' Terri's mouth formed a perfect circle for a second, her eyes wide. 'That must have been amazing!'

Amazing would have been one word for it. Keelin had a list of other, more heartfelt adjectives. 'It was certainly never boring.'

'I'm *so* jealous. Why can't we go to those places, Dad?'

'Because I have work and you have school. And anyway, stop complaining, you've been to London.'

'It's not the same as living there.'

When Keelin looked at Garrett's profile, she saw how his jaw clenched, just briefly. And she wondered why. Maybe his daughter's lack of travel experience was a source of greater debate with them? But surely he had to understand that, to a fourteen-year-old girl, the world must have looked like an adventurous, magical place?

Still, when he shot a cool glance her way, she felt she had to make amends somehow, or at the very least not add fuel to Terri's fire. So she looked for a safer topic instead and suddenly realized she'd been missing out on a major piece of information. And in not having asked had probably allowed Garrett his earlier, small indiscretion.

'Did you go to London on a school trip or did your mum and dad take you? Will she be at home when we get there? I'm looking forward to meeting her.'

The atmosphere in the car changed immediately.

But before Keelin could discover what she'd done wrong, they were pulling up at the house and Garrett was switching off the engine.

Keelin frowned in confusion as he scowled in silence at the steering wheel. And when she looked back at Terri, she just caught the tail-end of the look of pain she gave the back of her dad's head.

Before her eyes met Keelin's and she took a breath. 'My mum's dead. She died when I was little.'

Keelin's breath caught.

But before she could find something to say, Terri shrugged, unbuckling her seat belt before she reached for the door handle. 'And Dad doesn't like talking about her.'

'*Terri*—'

The softly warning tone went unheeded with another shrug. 'You can try if you like but I bet he won't say much about her. He never does.'

When she slammed the door shut, Keelin looked back at Garrett's profile, her voice low. 'I'm so sorry—I had no idea.'

'Why would you? It's not like we run around wearing T-shirts with it written on the front.' He shrugged in a similar way to his daughter. 'It was a long time ago.'

She waited until his face turned towards her, his eyes searching hers for a brief second while she held her breath, exhaling it on a question. 'You brought her up alone?'

'No, I brought her up with Dermot's help.'

'That can't have been easy.'

'No worse than being dragged from pillar to post most of her life might have been.'

Keelin looked down at her lap, joining her hands and focusing on them. 'We all have something to deal with.'

'Yes.' The word was low, intimate in the confined space of the car. 'Yes, we do.'

Keelin's eyes rose slowly, her gaze tracing up each of the buttons on his dark blue shirt, sweeping over the few dark hairs she could see at the open vee, and then up, past the sensual sweep of his mouth until it locked with his. The warm toffee melting as he blinked back at her.

And Keelin had never before been so knocked sideways. So aware of the steady sound of someone else's breathing, or the way that his mouth parted slightly as he took each breath, of how the very space that he occupied seemed made more *vibrant* by the very fact that he was in it.

Oh, this could *not* happen! Not with *him*.

But even as she straightened her spine and leaned back towards the door he turned away, his voice suddenly cooler.

'Dermot will be wondering what's keeping us.'

CHAPTER FOUR

'WHY do you call your father by his first name so much? Is that an island thing?'

Garrett tried to focus his attention on the mist-covered lane as they left the house, his grip tighter than necessary on the steering wheel. But the tension he felt wasn't linked to a fear of driving in such bad visibility. Oh, no. It had much more to do with being alone in Keelin's company. *Again.*

No matter how he tried he couldn't seem to stop himself from being abundantly aware of her, no matter how close or how far away she was from him. Even when she had sat on the far side of the living room after dinner, he had had to force himself to look away from her, to stop himself being consistently hypnotized by her smile or the golden sound of her laughter or her sweet scent when she walked by. A scent that now surrounded him inside his own car.

And he felt a growing resentment towards her for all those things. She had no damn business being so *noticeable.*

He frowned at her question. 'Do I?'

'Yes, I caught it a few times earlier but I guess I only really thought about it tonight.'

'Well, it *is* his name.'

'Would you like it if Terri called you Garrett?'

'No, I'm her dad, and I work harder on six days out of every seven to live up to that title; especially since she hit puberty.'

'You've earned it.' Her voice was softer this time, like velvet almost, as it reached across the minuscule gap between them and caressed his eardrums.

She had the most gorgeously sexy, husky voice. A bedroom voice. The kind of voice that would have seduced even without the aid of the way she looked. And she'd almost floored him when she'd walked into the foyer earlier. With her almost ethereal beauty, and an innocence that belied the kind of worldly upbringing he now knew she'd had.

'Don't you feel that Dermot has, too?'

Garrett could have corrected her simply enough. Dermot had more than earned it, which was why Garrett had taken his name in the first place. But his resentment at how he had been feeling in Keelin's company all evening, hell, since he'd first set eyes on her, translated as a lack of willingness to share any information with her.

'He's never complained, so maybe he's happy with it.'

With his eyes still fixed on the grey blanket beyond the windscreen, he couldn't attempt a look sideways to see her expression. But he felt the change, heard the slight whisper of the material of her dress against the seat as she straightened. And when she eventually spoke, her voice told him even more.

'Do you want to tell me what it is I've done wrong? Or should we just play twenty questions 'til I hit it? You can give me yes or no answers if that's easier for you.'

Her tone was cool, but there was an underlying edge to it that translated to him as hurt. Which brought an unwelcome wave of guilt washing over him.

'Is it because I mentioned Terri's mother earlier?'

'No, it's not because you mentioned Terri's mother.'

'Then what is it?'

His fingers flexed around the steering wheel. 'What makes you so sure you've done something wrong?'

'Maybe the fact that you've been staring at me with a scowl on your face for the last half an hour? You need to work some on your polite face, just for future reference.'

'Not all of us find it easy to bury things so deep that people can't see them. Or feel the need to try.'

He heard her sharp intake of breath and knew he'd hit a nerve. Well, at least all of his silent observation hadn't brought him to false conclusions, then...

Another risked, split-second sideways glance found her staring straight ahead, her full mouth pursed in a tight line. 'Which is what you try doing, isn't it? It's what you've been doing since I met you this morning.'

Keelin didn't answer him.

'I'm not the only one that needs to work some on their polite face. Just for future reference.'

She was silent for another long moment, then. 'And this *isn't* because I made the mistake earlier about your wife—you're quite sure about that? Because if it is then I apologize again, I had no way of knowing—'

'It isn't about that. And she wasn't my wife.'

'You didn't get married?'

'She wouldn't marry me. Marrying me would have involved her settling down and she wasn't ready to do that.' Now why had he just told her that? She didn't need to know. No matter how he tried he couldn't seem to stop himself talking around this woman. Or saying or doing something inappropriate, like offering a hug of comfort or his earlier comment about how 'good' he was...

And in telling her this latest piece of information he'd opened a doorway for further conversation on the subject, which was the last thing he wanted. 'It's about Terri if you really must know. I've spent all of her life making sure she had a secure home and firm foundation to build on. The last thing I need is for a stranger to come in and help feed her obsession with running off to the big city for a life of adventure.'

There was a long pause. Then. 'And you think one night with me will have her running off?'

'Well, you sure as hell didn't help. She's *fourteen!* She doesn't need some complete stranger making it out that the city is all things bright and shiny. And that's precisely what you did. It's tough enough keeping young people on the island as it is.'

'I had no intention of—'

'Maybe not, but you did.'

Another long pause, then. 'I see.'

Her voice was cooler this time and Garrett's resentment grew. This time because she was trying to hide the fact that she was hurt by his words. 'I don't expect you to understand my reasoning. I just ask that while you're here, you try and avoid the subject of how fantastic the city is—'

'Fine.'

When he risked another sidewards glance she turned away, focusing her gaze on the side window. And Garrett narrowly averted clipping one of the stone walls on either side of them, inwardly cursing the now-thick fog that brought his speed down to a crawl, prolonging the time he had to spend trapped in the car with her.

And yet there was still a part of him that felt he had to continue justifying himself. 'Living on a small island like Valentia can be tough enough for a teenage girl seeking fun and parties.'

'I get it.'

'And we've already been arguing for months about how much time she can spend with her friends off the island.'

'You've made your point, Garrett. You can drop it now.'

It suddenly occurred to him that he was trying too hard,

when he had no reason whatsoever to feel the need to smooth things over, did he? How he chose to raise his daughter had nothing to do with Keelin O'Donnell. He didn't need to seek her understanding, even if the fact that she now knew Terri had lost her mother too had seemed to create an instant understanding between them.

He had seen it the minute they'd gone inside the house. Had watched how Keelin seemed to be on Terri's wavelength without even trying. While he had spent the last year coming to terms with the fact that his little girl was growing up, finding her own feet, taking her first steps on a path that would inevitably take her away from him. Which had, in turn, led to a tension between them that had never been there before.

Maybe seeing her easy banter and instant friendship with Keelin had just reminded him of what he'd been gradually losing? She'd found it so easy to accept Terri as a young adult. Whereas Garrett still saw his little girl.

Add to that the fact that there were too many echoes in Keelin of the young woman who had left them and Garrett could pin his well-rounded resentment of her into a very definite square-holed lack of reasoning.

Keelin remained silent. And Garrett was glad she did.

But it didn't last. 'Have you considered trying to see it from her point of view? Trying to reach some kind of a compromise so that she doesn't end up hating you for keeping her from what she thinks she wants?'

Garrett clenched his jaw. 'And whose life are we talking about now?'

'Stop the car.'

'What?' He glanced her way and had to veer violently when he looked forward, swearing aloud as a result.

'Stop the damn car!'

'What the hell would I do that for? There's still a good

mile and a half to the village, not that I can see too far to confirm it!'

'If you don't stop this car this minute then I'm going to get out of it while it's still moving.'

'And go where exactly? You won't get ten feet in this!'

The interior light came on as she opened the door and, with another sharp expletive, Garrett slammed on the brakes.

'Don't you dare—'

But she was already out, before he had even yanked the handbrake into place. '*Keelin!*'

She appeared briefly in the arc of the headlights and Garrett swore a third time as he unclipped his seat belt and headed out after her. While he could still see her.

'You're being ridiculous, get back in the car.'

'Frankly I'd rather do my impersonation of a flying cow!'

Garrett lengthened his stride. 'If you don't get back in the car then in about two seconds I'm going *to put you* back in the car!'

Keelin stopped dead and swung on him. 'Oh, you could *try,* big guy!'

It was the most truly ridiculous challenge that had ever been aimed his way. And Garrett felt his mouth twitching as he looked at the dark outline of her against the fog.

'Come on, then, big guy.' The dark lines of her arms rose out from either side of her body. '*Make me.*'

The twitch developed into a full-blown smile. Lifting her up and throwing her over his shoulder would take so little effort. She was a little slip of a thing. But what she lacked in stature she more than made up for in guts.

He'd just bet she'd fight like a feral cat before she let him put her back in his car. So he'd have to try something else.

Folding his arms across his chest, he took a breath. '*Please* get back in the car.'

'No.'

He could practically hear her pouting. 'You're just going to wander around in this soup on an island you barely know? In the middle of the night.'

'I spent more than enough time this morning *stretching my legs* to know that this excuse for a road only goes to *one place*.'

'*And* the harbour.'

'Well, when my feet get wet I'll know to stop, won't I?'

'Bet you wish you'd brought those ridiculous wellingtons with you, then.'

He heard a noise that sounded distinctly like a growl.

Then silence.

And the impasse continued for several long moments. Until Garrett couldn't help himself, and a low chuckle escaped his lips. It was the most ridiculous situation he'd found himself in, in a while.

His reaction drew her darkened form closer to him, until he could see her scowling face in the grey light. 'Are you *laughing* at me?'

'No-o.' He schooled his features and shook his head.

She exhaled her answer. '*Liar!*'

'I'm laughing at the situation, that's all.'

'A situation *you* created!'

'I didn't ask you to get out of the car.' His amusement died and was replaced with another wave of frustrated anger. 'All I was doing was letting you know why I was scowling at you. You *asked*. I *answered*.'

Which wasn't entirely true. Well, the part about why he was scowling in the first place anyway. It was way more complicated. And that kind of honesty would only lead to an even bigger debate, one he could do without, frankly.

Keelin tilted her chin and glared up at him with eyes that were black in the dim light. 'What you were doing was being an inconsiderate son-of-a—!'

'Stop right there before this gets nasty.'

'Oh-h-h 'cos right now it's a Sunday school meeting, isn't it?'

'Keelin—'

Ignoring the warning edge to his voice, she pointed her arm past him. 'The cliffs are that way, I believe. Why don't you just go take a nice long running jump off one of them?'

She swung round again, managing to get two steps away before he reached for her arm. And once his fingers tightened around it, he spread his legs for a firm foundation and tugged, hard. So that she swung back round, her long hair flying out in an arc as she was hauled in against his body. Where he immediately wrapped his arms around her slight frame. And held on. Tight.

She fought like a feral cat.

When that didn't work she looked up at him with wide, dark eyes, her lips parted as she dragged deep breaths of much-needed air into her lungs. And her small breasts rose and fell against the wall of his chest. Where his heart thundered in response.

Never in all his born days had any woman had such an immediate, visceral effect on his libido.

She tilted her head to one side, carefully considering him as their joint, ragged breathing filled the silence.

And she smiled a slow smile.

In the soft light cast from the headlights, Garrett just about saw it, interpreting it as surrender before relaxing his arms around her in response. Man, she really was something, wasn't she?

On impulse, he wondered what she would do if he kissed her. Because for a mad moment he couldn't think of anything he wanted to do more...

But he didn't get a chance to find out.

Because it was then that the heel of her shoe slammed down onto his toes. *Hard.*

He released her, hopping back a step as he swore yet again. 'Damn it, woman!'

'If this bully-tactic method is an example of the way you deal with an argument, then it's not a bit of wonder your daughter is so keen to move away at the first opportunity she gets!'

Leaning his weight on his now aching foot, he stepped closer to her slight frame, towering over her as he lowered his face towards her upturned one, meeting her fiery challenge with steely determination. 'Get-in-the-car.'

Keelin folded her arms across her chest. 'Apologize first.'

'For being *honest* with you?'

'Oh, you weren't being honest with me, Garrett.' She laughed in his face. 'I think we're both aware of that.'

Garrett inwardly baulked. Was he that transparent?

'The truth is you don't like me much. I get that. What I don't get is why.' She took a breath. 'But to be *completely honest,* I don't actually care. I didn't come here to try and make you like me. I didn't even know you existed.'

'Then why *did* you come? Because that's the biggest mystery of all, isn't it?'

He saw her flinch from him. It was just about all he could see in the dim light, while standing so close to her, his large body placing hers in the shadows as he stepped closer. 'Come on, Keelin. You didn't just come here to leave back some letters. You could have parcelled them up and posted them from Dublin. So why *are* you here, *really?*'

It couldn't be just to make him insane in less than a single day…

The answer came out in an angry torrent. 'I came here to *meet* the man that wrote those letters! I came to try and understand what happened to make my mother leave someone who so obviously cared more deeply about her than any man since him! And, if you really must damn well know, I came to find out if he's my father!'

Garrett froze, the implication of her words sinking slowly into his brain as she stepped back from him, shaking her head as if she already regretted her angry outburst.

His voice softened as he stared at her. 'Dermot isn't your father, Keelin. I can tell you that for a fact.'

'You don't know that!' Her voice shook on the words. 'There's no way you could possibly know that for certain any more than I do.'

'Yes, I do.' He stayed rooted to the spot as he answered her in slow, careful tones. 'I know because I know Dermot, and he's not the kind of man who would ever have left a child of his in the world without knowing her father. It's not in him. And I know, because Dermot can't have children of his own.'

Keelin gasped. 'But he has *you!*'

'No, he doesn't. He married my mother when I was eleven. I took his name out of respect for him when I turned eighteen. Because he'd been such a good father to me. But he's not my father any more than he is yours, not in a blood sense.'

It took a long, tense moment before she spoke, her husky voice cracking on the words that ended in a whisper. 'That's why you keep calling him Dermot.'

'Yes.'

Garrett heard the soft moan the moment it left her lips. And he instinctively stepped forwards to reach for her, as he had at the gate that morning. 'Keelin—'

She avoided him, her voice a dull monotone when she spoke. 'I'd like you to take me back to the hotel now. I'm done with this island. There's no reason for me to stay here. Not one. Not now I've just made such a fool of myself.'

CHAPTER FIVE

'You don't want the room 'til the end of the week, then?'

'No, I want to check out.'

'And you won't be back again before the end of the week?'

'No, I won't be back at all.' Surely that was one of the reasons they called it 'checking out' as opposed to 'popping out'?

But Patrick's aged mother was quite persistent. 'We can get you a larger room if you'd like. Some people checked out this morning…'

Keelin was going to scream. She just really needed to leave, to get as far away from her embarrassment as humanly possible. Was that so much to ask for?

Instead she took a very deep breath. 'I don't want a bigger room. I *want* to pay my bill and leave.'

'Ah.' She squinted through her glasses at the credit card Keelin had set in front of her. 'Ah, you want to pay with a card. I'll have to get Patrick for that. I can't work that new machine he got. I'll be right back.'

Keelin watched with resignation as the older woman worked her way, incredibly slowly, from behind the desk and then across the foyer. What did a girl have to do to give someone money in this place? It had never been difficult anywhere else she had been in the world.

But even though a part of her really wanted to vent her frustration on someone, she couldn't bring herself to give out to the woman. The disaster was hardly her fault after all.

Keelin knew she'd been wrong to allow herself to set so much on her visit. *Very wrong.* It had been a lifeline at a time when she'd been floundering, was all. When she had needed a direction to focus her energies on.

It had seemed like fate at the time. When at the bottom of one of the huge trunks in the attic of her mother's Dublin house she had found the bundle of letters. Letters she had spent a full day reading, curled up on an old sofa the previous owner had left behind while she'd wept for what her mother had walked away from. For the poignancy of what could have been…

Following the letters had just felt like the right thing to do…

When in actuality she'd have been better taking a holiday somewhere nice and warm, with a beach and MaiTais and room service, where she could reflect and look forward. Where she could have decided what to do next and with the rest of her life…

With a sigh, she turned round and leaned back against the heavy wood reception desk, her eyes momentarily closing as she lifted a hand to rub at her aching temples.

'Keelin?'

When her eyes opened she saw Dermot in front of her. The man her mother had loved.

He smiled a little shyly. 'You *are* leaving, then.'

The fact that he had made it a statement rather than a question told Keelin what she needed to know and her stomach sank. She really had hoped to avoid this. 'You spoke to Garrett. He told you everything?'

'Yes, he told me everything. He thought I should know.'

She dearly wanted for the ground to open up and swallow her. Instead she dug deep, and managed a smile. 'It's not your fault, Dermot. I should just have written to you or something. It was silly of me.'

Dermot seemed to have nearly as much of a knack for reading her as the man who had become his son did. The man who had dragged a misconception from her and put her right.

His eyes flickered briefly and then he looked around, before searching her eyes again. 'May I talk to you before you go? I think maybe you still have some questions.'

'You really don't have to—'

'I know. But I'd like to.'

In the face of such genuine sincerity, Keelin couldn't really say no. And having talked to Garrett, Dermot was entitled to some answers himself, wasn't he? She just had to find a way of explaining it without sounding anymore pathetic than he probably already thought she was,

'All right.'

With a gentlemanly hand to the small of her back, he guided her through French doors and onto a paved section of garden at the back of the hotel. Then, at a wooden bench, he waited until she was seated, before sitting beside her.

Keelin glanced at him from the corner of her eye, more embarrassed than she could ever remember having felt. When he opened his mouth to speak, she spoke first. It was important he knew that he didn't need to feel responsible for what she had been blindly searching for.

'It's not your fault, Dermot, really. You have nothing to feel guilty about. I came here searching for something that wasn't here, that's all.'

'It was important to you.'

'Yes.' She frowned down at her hands where they lay on her lap. 'Yes, I guess it was. I just needed to know and now I do.'

'Did she never talk about him—your father?'

'Only to tell me I was more like him than her.'

'I don't think that's entirely true.'

Keelin flashed a small smile at him. 'There were times growing up when I might not have been so sure if I should have taken that as a compliment or not.'

'You should never doubt it's a compliment. She was an amazing woman; everyone who ever met her knew that. And I think you miss her very much, don't you?'

She couldn't allow herself to cry again; she really couldn't. She had done more than enough of that the minute she had closed the door to her room the night before, until she'd risen to take her shower in the early morning. Hot, heavy tears that she hadn't let go since the day her mother had told her she was dying. Tears she had held back while she'd put on a brave face as her mother had asked her to. Tears she hadn't even let go when she had died. Except for that one day with the letters.

But she'd let them out last night and she'd been emotionally drained afterwards. So she blinked hard to hold them back again. Especially in front of Dermot, who had done nothing to warrant the need to offer her comfort.

'Were you close?'

'Not in the traditional definition of the word for a long time. More so when she got sick. I stayed with her the last few months.'

'And you're a little lost without her, aren't you?'

An affirmative answer would only be half the story. Keelin had felt lost long before that. 'I guess when you spend your life with such a huge personality it's tough to know what to do when they're not there any more to offer advice. Even if you don't always agree with that advice.'

Dermot nodded in silent understanding. Then his larger hand appeared in Keelin's line of vision as he wrapped her clasped hands in it. One squeeze was all it took to get her to look at him.

'Did you read her letters yet?'

She faltered under his soft gaze. 'I started to—'

'But felt a bit like you were intruding?'

His smile eased her fear that his words were meant as a dig at his own letters. The ones she *had* read. But that wasn't what he meant. 'I didn't really know her all that well, I guess. She'd lived a whole life before she had me.'

Dermot chuckled. 'What child ever does know their parents as *people?* No matter what else they may be, or may have been through, we only ever see them as our parents.'

It was a good point. And unbidden, Keelin's thoughts turned to Garrett and his relationship with Terri. Was that part of their problem too?

Not that it was any of her business even wondering. He'd made it more than plain that she should just stay out of his daughter's life.

Dermot squeezed her hand again. 'You came here to find out a bit about your parents—'

'Well, one of them at least. But he's not here.' She smiled wryly. 'Much as I would have liked him to be.'

'I wish I could have told you it was me, Keelin. More than you could know. But it's not. Your mother was already pregnant with you when she got here. She just didn't know it until after she left. And she would never talk to me about him. Old love with a new one can be a difficult topic.' He leaned a little closer, his voice soothing and persuasive. And Keelin had a very brief glimpse of the man beneath the surface. The man her mother had cared about so long ago. There was a warmth, an intensity to him that reminded her again of Garrett. They might not have been blood relatives, but the similarity was there nevertheless.

'You might not have found your father here. But maybe you'll get a chance to find some of your mother. Stay a while, child. Take a walk in her shoes. This island has proved itself a great place to clear the mind for hundreds of people over the years and I think that maybe that's all you need: a chance to clear your mind, think things through. So stay. Come stay at the house if you'd like.'

Keelin laughed a little at that idea. 'I don't think that would go down too well with Garrett.'

'Ah, don't worry about Garrett. His bark is worse than his bite. And he's had his share of hard times along the way. He'll understand why you need some time. He's been there. And the island helped him to find his place.'

There was an echo in his words of the reassurances Garrett had made about Dermot when she'd first arrived. If he could just have managed to possess some of Dermot's understanding of other things then she might have felt better about how he'd feel about her staying. She'd already overstepped the mark in his eyes...

Nope. She couldn't stay at the house, there was no question about that. It would just be too awkward. Even the thought of bumping into him again felt awkward in advance. And it wasn't as if the island were that big a place. But Dermot's suggestion to stay and take some time was tempting. It had been so long since she had taken time just for herself.

Maybe that *was* what she needed above all else, regardless of the location. Time. *Time* to sort through her tangled thoughts and plan ahead.

She'd just have to find a way to avoid bumping into Garrett again. Since he'd made it so abundantly clear he didn't think much of her.

After Dermot left she stood at the reception desk and unwillingly, her thoughts strayed back to the argument the night before. Was there even such a thing these days as a parent/child relationship that was perfect? It made her wonder if her own teenage angst and run-ins with her mother had just been a different version of the same thing.

And she sighed.

Thing was, for a few brief hours, she had felt as if she were part of a real family. She had sat at a dinner table and joined in with jokes and conversation and warm company. And it had felt good. Better than good. Everyone had made her feel so at ease, so welcome. Except Garrett, who had changed as the evening had progressed, and who had eventually taken that fleeting sense of warmth and belonging from her by telling her to keep her distance.

It had hurt. Had hurt even before he'd taken the dream of being a part of that family from her, *for ever.*

Patrick came out from a room behind the desk. 'You wanted to check out?'

'No, actually, I'd like that bigger room.' She smiled sweetly. 'In fact, one without a ceiling that slopes right above the bed would be good. If I bump my head one more time…'

Garrett ducked down beneath the low doorway and focused on the steep steps into the tiny store. The one room, lined with shelves and able to accommodate about three people at one go, it constituted Knightstown's one and only place to buy things like newspapers and canned soup, the latter of which he had been sent to find.

But he didn't find soup. He found Keelin.

And when her eyes flickered upwards and locked with his he knew she wasn't exactly pleased to see him.

'I thought you were leaving?' He frowned as the unguarded words spilled out and her eyes narrowed in response. 'That came out wrong.'

She quirked an elegantly arched brow at him. 'You think?'

How did she *do* that? She was standing there dressed like a damn eighteen-year-old in a pink fluffy sweater, with her long hair in plaits, and she had managed to make him feel like a complete imbecile with two tiny words. Fully grown, successful, capable men weren't supposed to be so easily reduced to gibbering idiots. Well, in theory.

Even on the way back to the hotel the night before he had struggled to find words. But what could he have said?

His shoulders rose in defence. 'The last time I saw you, you were determined there was no reason for you to stay. If there'd been a ferry that late you'd have been on it.'

'I changed my mind.' She turned a radiant smile on the young lad behind the narrow counter as she paid for something that resembled a tourist map. And Garrett watched as the boy flushed in response before Keelin looked back at him with an icy glare. 'Women do that.'

'Oh, I *know.*'

She tilted her chin up and stepped towards him. But in the narrow aisle Garrett had the upper hand. She wasn't getting past him unless he wanted her to.

He was forced to look down at the top of her pale blonde head as she stared at the wall of his chest. Then, almost in slow motion, her head tilted back, long dark lashes rising until her large eyes locked with his.

And Garrett was momentarily lost for words.

How did she *do* that?

Her eyes narrowed in warning. And even though he knew she had to be wearing flat shoes, from the very fact that the top of her head barely hit his chin, he automatically moved his feet back a little.

Well, once bitten and all that…

Her throat convulsed as she swallowed. Then her brows arched upwards. So, after much deliberation, he stepped to one side. It was plainly obvious she had no desire to stand and chat a while. Which Garrett guessed he couldn't really blame her for, after his behaviour the night before.

In the narrow aisle, she had very little room to get past him.

Even with her slight frame, her body was still forced to brush against his. And Garrett felt the impact of it clean to his toes. His nose was invaded with a sweet hint of vanilla, static sparked where the wool of her sweater touched his, and he couldn't help it; his body jerked back.

Keelin hesitated for half a heartbeat. Glanced up at him with a look of pure venom that contradicted the brief flash of hurt in her wide eyes, then purposefully nudged his chest with her shoulder as she went past, the bell above the door heralding her exit.

While Garrett turned and stared at the closed door.

He pursed his mouth in annoyance as he thought. *She* probably thought he owed her an apology for the night before. She probably thought he had overreacted. *She* probably resented the fact that he had projected his anger at another woman who had left for the city onto her because she *came* from the city. Which would have been pretty damn petty after all…

It occurred to him that she couldn't possibly have known the latter. Which meant that, somewhere inside, he *knew* he owed her an apology, he *knew* he had overreacted, and he was all too aware of the fact that he *had* projected the hurt of old for the last woman who had floored him so fast onto the only woman who had done it to him since.

And Garrett Kincaid had never been known to be an unreasonable man. Before now.

Damn it!

She was standing on the corner when he came out, struggling her way through folding the huge map she had opened up, while a sharp inshore breeze tried to tug it from her hands.

'I maybe owe you an apology for last night.'

Keelin didn't even look at him. 'Yes, you do.'

Garrett gritted his teeth. She wasn't going to make it easy for him, was she? Of all the varying facets of Keelin

O'Donnell he had glimpsed since he had met her a little over twenty-four hours ago, this brusque, shut-people-out persona was his least favourite.

There was a sharper gust of wind, tugging the map up from Keelin's hand so she had to crumple it in against her breasts to keep it from escaping. Frowning hard, she tried to straighten it out again.

Garrett sighed. 'Where are you looking to go *this* time?'

'Straight to the house of the guy who designed this stupid map if I can't get it folded, actually.'

He felt a smile tug at his mouth. 'God help him.'

She glared at him again in response.

So he cleared his throat and forced the smile away. 'If you're going to be here a while we're bound to bump into each other.'

Keelin managed to force the errant map into uneven folds as she grumbled. 'Oh, goody.'

'And if we're going to bump into each other it would be nice to be able to be civil, don't you think?'

'Rather than ruin that supposed reputation you have for being a good guy?'

'I'm trying to smooth things over—' he leaned his head a little lower, his voice dropping a level '—just in case you hadn't got that part.'

His tone didn't endear him any and she raised her chin a very visible inch as she stared at him with a look that would have had Genghis Khan back down. But to Garrett, it had a very different effect.

His immediate gut instinct was, once again, to kiss her senseless. In the middle of the small main street, where the rumours would start so fast he'd be hearing about how they were getting married before he even made it home.

Which as a leading figure in the community he really

couldn't allow to happen. He didn't need several months' worth of knowing looks. Not again.

So wanting to kiss her so badly was a bit pointless. And yet the strongest need he'd felt in a long, long time. How did she *do* that to him? He was hardly some naïve seventeen-year-old any more!

A deep breath of cool, calming air, and an. 'I may have overreacted a little last night.'

He did his best to school his features so she didn't know how much the confession had cost him. Because a part of him, most likely the sensible part, didn't want to make up with her. It would have been an easier escape.

If there just hadn't been that brief flash of pain in her eyes in the shop…

Keelin studied him for what felt like an eternity. Then the hard glint in her eyes changed, softened slightly, the blue going a shade darker. 'You can't protect her from the rest of the world for ever, you know. I won't be the only person from the city she ever meets.'

Garrett clenched his jaw so hard his teeth hurt. 'I'm well aware of that. Thank you.'

More thoughts seemed to cross over her expressive eyes while he shoved his hands into his pockets and rocked back on his heels. He'd never met anyone that he could so clearly *see* thinking before. Windows to the soul. He had heard them called that. But he'd never looked into a pair of eyes that made him believe it so strongly.

Was there anything about this woman that didn't tug at him, drawing him in like the proverbial moth to an open flame?

She sighed loudly. 'But I guess if I had a child I'd want to keep them sheltered from the world for as long as I could, too. You only get so many years in your life to experience feeling safe and believing in things like the magic of possibilities.' Her long lashes fluttered against her creamy cheeks before she smiled a small smile up at him. 'So, even though you still haven't *actually* apologized out loud, this one time I'm prepared to let it go. It's not like I'll be here that long anyway.'

Garrett exhaled, felt the tension he'd been holding inside evaporate at the sight of that small smile, and the soft tone to her voice that spoke of a deeper understanding than even her words had communicated.

And he smiled in response. Simply because that was what he felt like doing.

After a moment she dragged her gaze from his and focused instead on the map. 'So do you want to make up to me some by telling me where I might find the lighthouse?'

Not renowned for his impulsive nature, Garrett surprised them both by answering with. 'Oh, I can do better than that. Let's call it my way of making up *properly* for being unreasonable.'

CHAPTER SIX

'ON THAT thing?' Keelin stared up at Garrett with wide eyes. 'Are you insane?'

His deep laughter made her insides flip over. How did he *do* that? She wanted so badly not to find everything he did or said so fascinating and so memorable. But, given the choice, most of all she wanted not to be aware of every minute physical movement, or of the fact that she could smell the musky base-tone of his aftershave when he was so close to her. He was just so *male*.

He leaned past her and she instinctively leaned away. Oh, Lord. How could one man have such an effect on her, even when she *knew* he wasn't overly fond of her? What sort of a cruel joke was that?

Not that a mutual attraction would have been any better. He hardly struck her as holiday romance material. Oh, no, he'd be the kind of man a woman would want to hold onto. And Keelin wasn't ready for a commitment that big.

Even so, the only senses she possessed that weren't currently experiencing everything that was Garrett Kincaid were touch and taste. And they both seemed to crave attention more than ever before.

As if in response to that thought, she folded her fingers into her palms and damped her lips with the end of her tongue. Maybe it would have been better if she'd not forgiven him so easily.

'It's easy. If you can drive a car then the theory carries through to driving a quad.'

As she stepped back a little to allow him access to the handlebars of the boy-toy he wanted her to drive her eyes were momentarily drawn to the outline of his rear in his jeans as he bent over. And she rolled her eyes heavenwards for a second. *Oh, c'mon, Keelin!*

She pinned a smile in place as he looked at her.

And he quirked a dark brow in response. 'Do you want to get on so I can show you how it works?'

'You're sure it's not just simpler to drive there? In a *car*? I could just follow you there…'

'Simpler *maybe*—' his eyes sparkled as he stood upright again, his dimples deepening '—but a lot less fun. Where's your sense of adventure?'

Keelin stared at him. 'It's true, isn't it?'

'What?'

'That men never actually grow up.'

'No, I wouldn't agree with that.' He took her hand and tugged her closer to the quad, still holding on while she swung her leg over the wide seat. 'We just need the occasional moment to take our minds off getting old and grey. Especially when we have teenage daughters who make us *feel* old and grey.'

Keelin would have made a comment about him being nowhere near either old or grey if she hadn't been completely distracted by his large hand holding hers. She'd held hands with men before, had gone *way beyond* holding hands as it happened. But even the way beyond of her experience didn't compare with the response holding hands with Garrett was evoking in her. His previous brief handshakes or helping hand had been nothing to this…

This time he had tangled his fingers with hers.

And it was such a large, warm, strong hand. With rough edges that hinted at his not having any problems with manual work and yet with a gentleness of touch that spoke volumes of control and thoughtfulness. So much information from one hand.

Would he be so controlled and thoughtful as a lover? Keelin would lay odds he would be. Whoever she was, she'd be a lucky girl!

The heat from that one hand took the chill from her smaller one, encouraged her without thought to curl her fingers back around his and just hold on for a moment. As if holding his hand were the most natural thing in the world. Something she had done every day of her life.

Oh-come-on! Whatever this was, it needed to stop.

She slipped free and wound her fingers around the handle-bars. 'All right, then, how does this stupid thing work? Though, just for the record, if I die falling off it, I'm haunting you for ever.'

It took ten minutes for her to be able to change gears smoothly. Which Garrett found highly amusing, of course. But it was his fault she was looking so ridiculous, his fault she still hadn't quite got her pulse down to a normal rate. His fault he had leaned over her body, his chest pressed against her back, while his warm breath tickled against her ear as he explained the theory of driving a quad in that multi-toned deep and husky voice of his—all of which had combined to raise her pulse to begin with!

So it wasn't until they hit the open fields and Keelin finally managed to co-ordinate her foot and her hands to change gears smoothly that she began to have *fun*.

And with the wind in her face and the quad bouncing beneath her, she shook her head and laughed aloud.

'That's it!' His yelled voice sounded over the roar of the engines. 'You've got it!'

Keelin looked over at him briefly as he matched his own quad to her pace and she grinned at the mixture of amusement and pride on his face. Oh, she'd got it, all right. She'd got it bad for someone there was absolutely no point getting it bad for.

Déjà-vu, her mother would have said…

She watched as he gunned the engine and sped ahead of her, glancing briefly over his shoulder to make sure she was keeping up.

Well… Keelin O'Donnell might have been many things, but she wasn't a quitter…

She laughed aloud again. This really was insane.

It was as well he slowed down before the edges of the cliffs. Because Keelin had had so much fun bumping over hill and dale to try and catch up with him that she might not have noticed she had to stop.

By the time she parked beside him, he had already swung one long jean-clad leg over the seat and was looking out over the expanse of grey-blue ocean, the large white lighthouse a backdrop behind him.

So, with her engine shut off and everything turned to neutral that she could remember being told about, Keelin looked upwards in the same direction as him. And her breath caught in a gasp of awe.

Garrett smiled beside her. 'Yeah, not bad, is it?'

She aimed a brief, full blown smile at him. 'You are officially the King of Understatement. It's sensational.'

'We may be lacking in some of the amenities of the big city, but we make up for it with the views.'

Dragging her gaze away from the splendour of sky and open ocean that stretched out in a panorama before her, Keelin studied Garrett's profile, eventually asking. 'You have a real thing about the city, don't you?'

'I wouldn't be a big fan, no.'

'Any particular reason or are you just a good old country boy at heart?'

Without turning his head, he glanced at her from the corner of his eye, the breeze lifting his fringe of dark chocolate hair and pushing it across his forehead. '*Definitely* a country boy at heart. But I tried the city. We didn't get along. Too many people walking past each other and never looking to see who's there for my liking.'

He had a point.

But they could also be vibrant, exciting, vital places to live, with a wealth of diversity in people and areas, a heartbeat of liveliness that never seemed to completely die down, even in the small hours of the morning…

Whereas, beautiful as it might be, surely a place like this could be as lonely, if not lonelier, than the city, especially in the winter?

'Any place has its good and its bad. It's what each individual makes of it that decides whether or not it's home to them.'

This time he did turn his face towards hers, a half-smile on his sensual mouth. 'That's very philosophical.'

Keelin leaned back a little and swung a leg over the seat so that she was facing him, before folding her arms. 'You really can be very patronizing when you want to be, can't you?'

'Can I?' He folded his arms in a mirror of her stance.

Keelin nodded. 'Yes, you can.'

'And you can be very outspoken. You don't say something just to pass yourself, do you?'

'Not any more I don't. I used to have to smile at people 'til my cheeks hurt. Now I figure I don't have to do anything if I don't want to.'

He hesitated for a brief moment. 'Who made you do things you didn't want to do?'

'Everyone.' She smiled, glancing out to sea for a brief

second before she shrugged her shoulders and looked back at him. 'Okay, maybe not everyone. But there were times when it felt like it was.'

'And why did they want you to keep smiling?'

'Oh, it's the full-time job of the children of all the rich and famous, didn't you know? We're born to it. And we either rebel or we do as we're told. I chose the latter, eventually.'

'Was your mother famous?'

That produced a burst of instantaneous laughter. 'Hell, yes, didn't Dermot mention that part?'

Garrett silently shook his head, his gaze steady.

And Keelin found she couldn't keep looking into the intense light in his eyes. It was as if he could see right through her, past the bright smile pinned to her face and all the way to that deeply hidden place inside her that had lived in the shadows for so long. She didn't want to show that kind of weakness in front of this man, didn't want him to know how lost she still felt a lot of the time, even at this point in her life.

She swallowed hard as she watched a cresting wave make its way to shore. It was strange, meeting someone who didn't know her mother, or at least know *of* her. There had been times in Keelin's life when she had felt the whole world did. And that she was invisible.

'What was she famous for?'

Keelin continued watching waves. 'She was a painter. A fairly outspoken one, as it happens. TV, lectures, guest appearances at galleries—all the trappings of fame with her glamorous friends and jet-set lifestyle.'

'And a daughter who hated every minute of it.'

Keelin shot him a meaningful glance. 'Not every child wants the lifestyle their parent chooses for them. We all have to find our own place in the world eventually.'

'*Touché.*' He inclined his head.

She studied him with narrowed eyes. 'You're a bit unusual for a farmer in the middle of nowhere, aren't you?'

'Because I happen to know one word in French?' His mouth twitched.

'No.' She unfolded her arms and waved a hand at him. 'There's just something about you that doesn't scream clichéd sheep-herder at me.'

'Snob.'

She searched for, and found, the teasing light in his warm eyes and smiled in response. 'Well, you're just not.'

'I'm not sure how I should take that.'

'Don't get excited; it's not meant as anything other than an observation.'

'From your wide and extensive knowledge of the kind of people who keep sheep?'

'All right.' She inclined her head as he had. 'Maybe from my preconceptions as a city girl about the kind of people who *might* keep sheep for a living.'

He smiled again. '*Snob.*'

Keelin laughed. 'All right, how would I know what kind of a person keeps sheep? I just wouldn't expect someone like you to do nothing *but* keep sheep for a living.'

A flush was already creeping up her cheeks before he answered. 'I'm sure there's a compliment in there somewhere.'

Looking back out to sea, she murmured. 'There was.'

A deep burst of laughter was blown across to her ears by another gust of wind. But he didn't say anything. So, eventually she looked back at his profile and waited until he turned to meet her gaze again.

He took a deep breath. 'I should just let you feel bad for a while on behalf of sheep farmers everywhere. But I don't just keep sheep for a living. I do a bit more than that. In fact, the island relies on me doing a bit more than that. Though, just to bring you down a peg or two, I wish I could have proved you wrong. Farming, in all its varying forms, is what has kept this country of ours going for centuries.'

'I'm aware of that.' She frowned at the lecture, and at the very fact he'd needed to hand it out. 'I just can't seem to say anything right around you, can I?'

'I'd imagine that's pretty frustrating for someone who's probably been trained to say the right thing at the right time for most of their life.'

'Yes, as a matter of fact, it is.'

Garrett nodded slowly. Then looked back out to sea.

And Keelin honestly wanted to go over and push him off his perch. He was the most annoying person she had ever met. She opened her mouth to say as much and then shut it. It wasn't as if she was faring too well in the conversation department, was it?

Thing was, for a brief moment, while being taught the workings of a quad and then chasing across the fields together, she had felt that they were getting on a little better. That maybe he didn't completely dislike her. After all, this little jaunt had been his idea…

And the thought of him not hating her hadn't felt too damn bad, as it happened.

'So, you never rebelled?'

Her brows dropped into a frown of confusion as he looked across at her. 'What?'

'You said that the children of famous people either rebelled or did what they were told. You never felt the need to rebel?'

The frown disappeared and was replaced by a mischievous smile. 'Ah, now, I never said *that*.'

Garrett's mouth curled into a full blown smile that teased out his dimples. 'What did you do?'

'Which time?'

'How many times were there?'

'A few.'

'So, what did you do?'

Keelin couldn't help but notice how he slowed the words into an almost seductive drawl, how he leaned his head a little more in her direction, how the warmth in his eyes became a shade darker in challenge. And away went her pulse again.

So she damped her lips with the end of her tongue before she answered. 'No, you see you already have a low enough opinion of me, what with thinking I'm a snob, and my little transgression on the subject of sheep farming—'

'And saying it that way doesn't make it any better. You still sound like a snob.

'Okay, then. So teach me something about farming so I know better.'

'*You* want to learn about farming?' His face said he didn't quite believe that.

And Keelin felt it was about time he had his opinion of her changed. If she did nothing else before she left this place she would show him a book couldn't be judged by its cover. 'I've always believed if you don't learn something new every day, then it's a day wasted.'

'Your flowery wellingtons wouldn't last five minutes on a real working farm.'

Her chin lifted. 'My flowery wellingtons are ready to prove you wrong.'

'They won't be so flowery when we're done.'

'Maybe they don't care as much about outer appearances as you like to think they do.'

'Oh, really?'

'You're just afraid I'll turn out to be absolutely amazing as a sheep farmer and prove you wrong.'

'That won't happen.'

'Well, we'll see, won't we?'

Garrett shook his head and then made a lie of the movement. 'Yes, we will.'

It was a very small victory. But Keelin grinned nevertheless.

He turned his face away and looked up at the large light-house that stood on the cliffs behind him. 'So, you want to go look at the lighthouse a little closer or are we done looking at tourist attractions?'

Keelin stood up and walked a little closer to him, her voice dropping as she looked over his head. 'Oh, I didn't come here to see it 'cos it was a tourist attraction…'

And then she walked past him, her eyes rising to study the polished glass of the circular windows at its peak.

Garrett watched her walk past, a small scowl of confusion on his face as he turned his head to keep watching. Before he gave in and pushed up onto his feet to follow her. 'Then why *did* you want to see it—just to fill in some time?'

She leaned her head towards him when he was by her side, still not looking at him, and answered him in a stage whisper. 'This was where Dermot first kissed my mother.'

'It is?'

Keelin nodded, tilting her chin as she thought. 'Uh-huh. It sounded romantic, so I thought I'd come take a look at it to see for myself.'

She didn't see Garrett's throat convulse as he swallowed, her gaze instead moving back to the ocean, taking it all in as she stopped walking. Then she closed her eyes and breathed in a deep breath of the salty air, which she exhaled on the words, 'And it is.'

Her eyes flickered open, her chin rising so she could look up at him as his eyes met hers. 'I guess you've just got to be here with the right person.'

He blinked a couple of times, his answer slow and measured. 'I guess so.'

Keelin nodded again. 'You'll have to keep it in mind, then, as a place to come to with someone you actually like.'

The gaze he gave her was consuming as he looked back and forth into each of her eyes, then swept lower, over her nose, and finally to her mouth, before looking back up again with a small smile. 'Oh, I don't believe I've ever said I didn't like you. Liking you isn't the problem.'

Keelin couldn't breathe, her voice coming out low and husky. 'It isn't?'

'Nope.' He shook his head, oh, so slowly, his gaze still steady and the small smile still in place. 'I like to wait and get to know someone better before I make a judgment call. Maybe you should try doing the same thing.'

And with that he turned away and walked back to his quad. Which left Keelin staring in amazement at his broad back.

Garrett thought she didn't like him? *Really?*

If only he knew…

CHAPTER SEVEN

KEELIN was so absorbed in the story unfolding in her mother's side of the letters that she didn't notice the noise level rising in the hotel until the music kicked in, the heavy beat seeming to come up through the floor into her feet.

And folding the letter she'd been reading back into its envelope, she looked around the dining room, finally noticing she was alone.

There had been at least four tables full when she'd come in for dinner. So where had everyone gone? Even the young waiter who had hovered over her table as she ate seemed to have disappeared into thin air, and he'd been like a loyal puppy every mealtime since she'd arrived.

By the time she walked into the foyer, she discovered where everyone had migrated to and that most of the island's inhabitants seemed to be flooding through from the bar where the music originated from.

'Well, hello, pretty lady.'

She glanced up at the burly, ruddy-faced man who stepped into her pathway, and aimed a small, polite smile at him. 'Good evening.'

'Are you here for a wee visit, then?' He glanced around him. 'Not here on your own, surely?'

Keelin tried sidestepping. 'Yes, I'm just here for a few days.'

The man sidestepped in front of her, blocking her way. 'On your own? A pretty wee thing like you shouldn't be left on her own. Come and join the party sure; everyone's welcome, you know.'

'Thank you, but no. I've had a long day, and I'm not exactly dressed for a party.'

'Well, you look gorgeous to me.'

'She's too young for the likes of you, Michael.' Another, younger man appeared by his side. 'Let someone more her age get her up to dance. You'd like a dance now, wouldn't you, miss?'

Not with someone who looked as if they'd barely left school, *no*. Keelin couldn't help but notice how a small crowd seemed to be forming around her. The island really must have had a lack of single, available women, if one was given so much choice in the space of a few minutes.

It was actually quite flattering, in a way. But she was still a woman travelling alone. And, capable as she was of looking after herself, up against a crowd of large men she wasn't sure she would fare so well if she had to physically fight them off.

She'd just have to try charm instead. So she pinned a confident smile in place to cover her rapidly developing sense of claustrophobia and lifted her chin. 'Now, fellas, really, you can't tell me there's not plenty of girls in the bar who'd love to dance with a bunch of good-looking men like you…'

Garrett pushed through the foyer doors and looked up to find Keelin holding court in the centre of the room.

And the shaft of anger that cut through him almost had him turn round and walk straight back out. It was none of his damn business what she did or who she flirted with. But somehow that didn't make seeing it any less infuriating.

His eyes roamed over the group surrounding her, recognizing every one by name. And immediately knowing there wasn't anyone there who would prove a threat to her. But there was no way *she* could know that.

Surely with her worldly experience she should know better? And these boys would all be drinking and would get rowdier as the evening progressed. *Had the woman no sense?*

'Hello, Garrett, there's a good crowd in for John's do, isn't there?'

He forced a smile onto his face for Patrick's wife. 'Aye, there is, Shona. Any excuse for a night out, right?'

Shona laughed. 'Aye, good for business, though.'

Garrett smiled a more genuine smile as she winked at him and lifted a tray from the reception desk. Then, as she moved away, his eyes moved back to where Keelin's hand was being taken by Paul Logan, one of the local lotharios.

Garrett gritted his teeth.

One drink to show his face and he was out of here. He didn't need to stand and watch her put all of her city-girl confidence to good use.

But as he walked across the room towards the bar, from his peripheral vision he noticed her face turn in his direction. And when he looked over she smiled.

Even from a few paces away he could see the silent plea for help, as if she had some kind of silent way of communicating that he could immediately understand.

Paul tugged on her hand again, and when Garret saw her trying to extricate it, and getting nowhere fast, he knew he really had no choice. And all his good intentions to keep wagging tongues on the island still went right out the window...

'There you are, sweetheart.' The small crowd parted like the Red Sea as he got closer. 'Sorry I'm late.'

One steady glance at Paul was all it took for the younger man to release Keelin's hand and step back.

And Keelin's smile grew in response. 'Just so long as you're here now, darling.'

Darling? The word rolled off her tongue like an outgoing tide off sand, as if she used the word on him every day of the week. But another glance into her eyes told him in that silent language of hers that she was just playing along. So he took the invitation to move closer and leaned down to place a brief kiss on her soft cheek, before he settled his hand possessively against her back and looked around at her sea of admirers.

'Great crowd in tonight, isn't there, boys?'

There was a chorus of varying 'Ayes' and 'That there is' as they all shifted their attention from Keelin and onto Garrett. Then Paul, his cheeks warm, laughed a little nervously and announced, 'That's a fine-looking girl you have there, boss. Where you been hiding her?'

Garrett's hand smoothed along the silky material on Keelin's back until he circled her shoulders with his arm, drawing her slight frame in against him. And his breath caught for a moment as she turned, relaxing in against his side and raising a small hand to rest against his chest.

Glancing down, he found her looking up at him with shining eyes, her long lashes flickering against her cheeks in lazy blinks of heavy eyelids. Oh, she was *good* at the 'let's pretend', wasn't she?

If he didn't know better he'd have been convinced that they had more than a two-day 'relationship'. In fact, as her hand smoothed back and forth against his chest, he'd even be convinced that their relationship was one on a *much* more intimate level.

She ran the pink end of her tongue over her lips and smiled as her gaze focused on his mouth. 'Garrett's been showing me the island, haven't you, darling? We found the sweetest spot up by the lighthouse earlier...*very* romantic.'

Garrett felt his whole body tense at the innuendo.

There was a low whistle from one side and Garrett shook his head slightly as he looked back at their audience. 'What can I say, boys? She's been keeping me busy with all that sightseeing.'

'Are you from Killarney, then?'

Keelin continued to let her fingertips move against Garrett's chest as she sidled a little closer to him and turned her head to answer Michael. 'A little further afield than that. I'm based in Dublin at the minute. Just here for a visit, like I said.'

All eyes seemed to stare at Garrett.

Before Michael reached out to pat his back and lowered his voice so that Keelin had to strain to hear him. 'Hope this one goes a bit better, boss. We'd all be mighty pleased for you.'

As the group gradually dispersed Keelin felt Garrett's arm loosen on her shoulders and she turned her face round a little to look back at his face. He, in turn, looked down at her with hooded eyes.

She frowned in confusion. 'What did he mean by 'this one going better'?'

He took a step back from her and shook his head. 'It's old news.'

'Not to me, it's not.'

Wide shoulders shrugged. 'It doesn't matter. Do you want a drink now that I'm here? The party has an open invitation for everyone.'

Keelin studied him for a long moment, not prepared to allow it to slide that easily. And with a sudden insight, it made sense to her. 'Did Terri's mother come from the city? Is that why you're so against it and against her wanting to leave?'

She knew she'd got it right when he couldn't hold her gaze, when his jaw tensed for a brief moment. 'Like I said, it's old news.'

Oh, no, she wasn't that easily distracted. 'How did you meet her?'

Garrett seemed to take a long time to decide whether or not

to tell her. And just when she thought he would brush it off, he surprised them both by confiding. 'Her family was originally from Dublin, but they had a holiday place here. They eventually made the move when she was the age Terri is now and they wanted somewhere healthier for her to grow up. But she never settled, couldn't wait to get back to all the *action*. That action eventually took her to a late-night party she left blind drunk and she walked out in front of a car. She was two weeks away from her twenty-first birthday.'

'Where was Terri?'

'With a teenage babysitter in a tiny little bedsit. She was eight months old.'

Keelin stared at him, floundering for the right words to ease the bitterness she heard in his voice, until he cut her short by asking again. 'Do you want that drink?'

'Yes, yes, that would be nice. Thank you.' And Keelin honestly felt as if she needed one.

Any wonder he worried so much about Terri wanting to go back to the city. He must have had a hundred different horrific scenarios in his head as a parent after what had happened to her mother. And, regardless of the odds of any of them happening, being the kind of man he was, he probably thought it better to lower the odds to zero by stopping her from ever going.

Keelin might even have felt the same way in his shoes. But had he talked to Terri about it? Explained his fears to her? It might have helped some…

With his hand once again on the small of her back, he guided them towards the packed bar. While Keelin thought over the new information.

Keelin's mother might have had her faults, but she had never left her child in the early years, not to run off and have wild parties. Even when Keelin had been in full-time education she had set up a house nearby so that Keelin could come home from school every night and have some sense of routine. Erratic as that routine might have been.

It had only been in school breaks and as she'd got older that their life had become more nomadic—the source of many of their arguments as Keelin had rebelled against having to behave all the time in front of her mother's famous friends and the press that her mother had courted. But even then, she had still wanted Keelin nearby. And she had relied on it from when she'd first found out she was sick until the very end.

Keelin had only known Garrett for such a short amount of time, and yet she knew instinctively that he would never have abandoned his infant child either, *especially* for wild parties. He wouldn't have put anything ahead of her care and safety. Keelin just *knew* that about him.

Maybe Terri's mother just hadn't been ready for the responsibility, hadn't had it in her to give up the adventure of youth. But her selfish pursuits had cost her dearly in the end.

Had Garrett still loved her then? How had he coped with her loss and taken on the care of a baby at the same time when he had still been so young himself?

Everyone in the bar seemed to greet him as they pushed their way through. Some even made the old-fashioned greeting of touching the peak of an invisible cap with their forefinger. And they *all* called him 'boss'. Which brought another piece of information recently learned into the forefront of Keelin's mind.

Garrett had said the island relied on him being more than just a sheep farmer, hadn't he?

When he found them a space at the bar, she stood up on tiptoe to call into his ear. 'They all keep calling you boss. Do you employ *everyone*?'

Garrett turned his face towards her and smiled a more genuine smile than he had since he'd come to her rescue. 'Little old sheep-herder me?'

Still on tiptoe, her face close to his, she laughed. 'All right, I deserved that.'

'Yes, you did.'

The nod of his head and the firm tone of his words were diluted by the warmth in his eyes. And, still on tiptoe, Keelin found she couldn't stop smiling at him. It had been a long time since she'd met someone who could put her in her place so easily, who could take her usual perceptive knack for correctly pigeon-holing people and knock it right on its heel.

'Let's start again, shall we?' She leaned back a little and managed to bring her hand up between them, her eyes fixed on his. 'Keelin O'Donnell, daughter of famous-artist mother, learning rapidly not to be so judgmental and to try asking questions before she jumps to conclusions or puts her foot in it.'

Garrett laughed and shook his head, glancing past her for a second before he extended his own hand and circled her fingers in his. 'Garrett Kincaid, stepson of a man who I think is more pleased you came here than he'd admit, promising to try not to judge you based on the one woman I ever knew like you before I know you better.'

Keelin made one firm up-and-down shake before she untangled her hand from his. 'See, that wasn't so tough really.'

'You think?' Motioning to Patrick's wife behind the bar, he leaned his head closer again to ask. 'What do you want to drink?'

'White wine would be lovely, thanks.'

Drinks in hand, he guided them expertly through the crowd again until they were on the periphery, where they wouldn't have to stand so close, or raise their voices to speak. And despite their mutually agreed 'new beginning', Keelin suddenly felt ridiculously shy in his company.

Not that she was some kind of *femme fatale*. But normally she was more confident with people, more in control of her surroundings. She knew what topics to use as small talk to break the ice, could think of varying subjects to strike up a conversation. Years of socializing with the varying different people who surrounded her mother had taught her that.

Yet with Garrett her mind was suddenly blank. As if the part of her that had got so many things wrong with him before was reluctant to make the same mistakes again, so decided it was safer to just say nothing at all.

Instead, she became a silent observer as people came over to speak to him. And within twenty minutes she was smiling broadly.

As the latest group of visitors moved away he turned towards her, his eyes narrowed in suspicion. *'What?'*

'You're the male version of me.'

His dark eyebrows rose in question.

So Keelin continued. 'You know exactly what to say to people in the right social setting. How to brush them off politely when you don't want to talk to them any more, who needs encouragement to talk…'

He took a moment to mull that over. Then moved his head from side to side as he teased. 'And yet when you talk to *me* it's not that easy for you, is it?'

'No. I seem to spend a lot of time in your company putting my foot in my mouth or behaving completely out of character.' She held her breath after the words spilled out. It was one hell of a confession. It gave him a hint of how he unsettled her. Which might lead to him asking why. And she didn't really want him to know why.

'And why do you think that might be?'

Yep, there it was. Now, how best to answer that one? There was the honest answer, the one that could be laid firmly at the door of physical attraction. The attraction that had been there since he'd first walked out of the mist. But there was also the fact that *since* he'd walked out of that mist two days ago she had gone from attraction to anger to humiliation to embarrassment and back to attraction in varying degrees and on varying occasions. To the point where it felt that she had left her usual personality at the ferry terminal on the mainland before she'd even got to the island.

But that could be because of everything else she was dealing with, couldn't it? Nothing in her life was 'usual' any more.

Where realistically did she even begin to try answering his question without embarrassing herself again by making a confession that could lead nowhere or opening herself to his pity by admitting she hadn't much of a clue about anything any more?

Garrett watched her while she thought over his question, a dozen differing thoughts seeming to cross over her eyes while she lifted a hand to brush a long length of silken hair behind her ear. Her other hand swirled the wine in its glass almost absent-mindedly, while she avoided his gaze and looked around the room.

They might have made an attempt at a new beginning at the bar, but it hadn't removed any of either of their barriers of mistrust, had it? And it was as plain as day to him that she had as many as he did. But did he automatically think that because he had opened up to her a little that she should do the same? It wasn't as if he had wanted to tell her in the first place.

But he'd put it out there now. And he *did* want to know about her. 'Am I that scary? It's not like you ever have to set eyes on me again after a week or so, or however long it is you've decided to stay.'

The smile she gave him didn't quite make it all the way up into her expressive eyes. 'I haven't decided how long to stay. But I can hardly hide here for ever.' She paused and took a deep breath, glancing away from his face and then back again. 'And, yes, actually, you can be a little scary, now that you ask.'

Garrett chuckled at her honesty. 'Why?'

Her narrow shoulder shrugged and she focused her gaze on

her glass, swirling its contents again. 'You're very in control of yourself. I guess that reminds me that I'm not.'

If she thought that then he'd obviously done a pretty good job of hiding how out of his control zone he'd been since he'd met her. That was something. But her answer raised another question. 'And why aren't you in control?'

This time the smile was sad, her gaze skimming up to lock with his only briefly, but long enough for him to see the deeply felt pain there.

'I have no idea what I'm doing any more.'

'Because your mother is gone and you don't have to look after her?'

'Partly that. It's a full-time, emotionally draining job looking after someone who's terminally ill, even with a *Macmillan* nurse to help out. But saying I have no control of my life without my mother makes it sound like I couldn't do anything without her influence, and that's not true either. But when she was here I was always aware that everything I did and said was a reflection on her in some way. I had a, duty of sorts, as her daughter. Or at least I always felt I did.'

Garrett involuntarily felt his feet carry him a step closer to her side, his voice lowering. 'Didn't you have a duty to yourself too?'

Her long lashes swept upwards and her eyes locked with his. But she didn't say anything. She just searched his eyes, her mouth parting an almost minuscule amount.

And Garrett found himself focusing on her mouth, on the bowed sweep of her lips and the deep pink colouring that made it look as if she had recently been thoroughly kissed. He felt the control she thought he had slipping again as the primal urge to kiss those lips leaned his head a little closer to her.

But he managed to stop himself, instead looking into her eyes as he asked in a husky voice. 'A duty to be happy at least? Are you happy, Keelin?'

Keelin damped her lips before answering, her voice barely audible. 'I'd like the chance to be. I don't know that anyone can really ask for more than that.'

CHAPTER EIGHT

KEELIN was creeping underneath his skin. Garrett knew it as surely as he knew there was no point to it happening. Yet there was a certain exhilaration to it too, a sense of awareness that, he realized at some point after she had gone back to her room and he had made his way home, he had missed in his life without realizing he was missing it.

Had he been so absorbed in building a life for himself on the island? One he could be proud of. One that gave back to the community he had grown up in. One that would secure a future for Terri. That at some point he had shut himself off to the sheer exhilaration of feeling a deep-seated awareness of a woman, that kind of attraction that was beyond his control? That thrill of anticipation in the 'chase'?

Not that he'd been celibate for over a decade either…

But nothing had compared to the tremor of anticipation he felt at seeing Keelin again. Despite the voice in the back of his head that kept telling him he should back off.

She was just a city gal taking a little holiday in the country, after all. Taking a break to get her thoughts gathered together and find a new direction now that she was missing the larger-than-life character that had been her mother. She was finding her feet, and then she'd go back to the life she had waiting for her in the city; wherever that city might eventually prove to be in the world.

It didn't really matter where it was. It wouldn't be anywhere near Valentia Island. She really wasn't born to be a country girl.

But even though she wasn't much of a country girl, some things she knew straight off when he brought her to the home farm.

'Those aren't sheep.'

Garrett's face stayed completely straight, despite the immediate spark of amusement he felt growing **in his** chest. 'What gave that away for you?'

'Ooh, let's see…'

He had a huge inner fight to keep his laughter at bay when she lifted a hand and tapped one long, slender finger against her pouting mouth as she pondered her answer.

'I never actually said I kept sheep. You just assumed I did.'

Her gaze swept upwards and locked with his, a sparkle of amusement in their blue depths as she removed her finger to speak. 'And you *let me* assume.'

'No, I just didn't correct you.'

'Same thing, don't you think?'

'It seemed an awful shame to break the news to you that you weren't right about everything when you were so determined you were. And you said you wanted to learn about farming; you weren't specific on the animal.'

The sparkling increased. 'Mmm, and you've had such a problem setting me straight on things since we met, haven't you? You're very behind the door that way. You couldn't have just mentioned the lack of sheep in passing?'

'I did tell you, you wouldn't end up a better sheep farmer than me. I just didn't mention that was because I don't keep sheep. And anyway, men like to be able to pick and choose their battles; it's an age-old thing.'

And with Keelin it seemed better to choose ones he could

win. As it was he was already losing the war when it came to keeping his distance from her and playing it safe.

Keelin cleared her throat, focusing forward as she rolled up the sleeves of her thick sweater. 'All right then, what are we doing with them?' A frown appeared in the form of a vertical crease between her arched brows as a thought occurred to her. 'Please tell me we're not *milking* them?'

A chuckle escaped from low in his throat. 'Well, actually—'

She stared up at him. 'We're not, are we?'

His hand reached out to guide her forwards, but he managed to stop it before it made contact with her back. The whole 'reaching out and touching her' thing really needed to stop. That thought had occurred to him the night before, too. He'd never been known for being a tactile man, before. Not with anyone but his daughter. And even *she* had been shunning that in public for the last year or so.

Maybe the fact that Keelin was so slight and delicate reached out to the part of him that was missing that kind of contact. That sense of protectiveness.

If he could just make himself see her as anything other than a fully grown, beautiful woman who tugged at him constantly with some kind of invisible thread...

'Well, if you don't think the flowery wellingtons are up to it...'

She continued walking by his side, looking at him from the corner of her eye. 'The wellingtons are all for learning a new skill... It's not about that. It's just that there are—' she stopped at the front of the large shed and waved an arm in front of her '—*millions* of them. I wasn't exactly planning on staying for the next year.'

They stood side by side and looked at the long rows of pens down either side of the immaculate barn. Where loud mooing greeted them.

'A hundred, give or take. Not millions.'

The rows seemed to stretch out for miles to Keelin's eyes. And much as she wanted to impress this man with her ability to take anything on, she faltered.

When another chuckle of deep laughter reached her ears, she turned her face and tilted her chin to look up at him. And found her pulse misbehaving as it had the night before when his head had briefly descended towards hers.

'All right.' She sighed as she looked forwards. 'You win this round.'

'The wellingtons concede defeat?'

'The wellingtons are still prepared to learn, but they might get a bit tired after the first fifty and the milk could go off in the others before we get to them.'

'Just as well for the wellingtons that we have an almost automated milking service here then—' he stole one last look at her face before walking into the shed '—and that they were all milked over an hour ago. There's a team of four here full time.'

She caught up with him inside three steps, frowning a little. Half irritated that he'd yet again outwitted her and allowed her to make herself look stupid, and half amused that he'd done it so easily and with a twinkle of gentle amusement in his eyes.

'Well, if milking isn't the lesson then we're not done. The wellingtons refuse to concede.'

'Ah, but the wellingtons already did. They can't take it back now.'

'You play dirty.'

'If that's what it takes.' He nodded.

They continued side by side while Keelin felt her frown disappear, a smile twitching at the corners of her mouth when he glanced at her again with the twinkling still evident in his warm toffee eyes. All right, she quite liked that she'd put that twinkling there.

'You're smiling.' He stated the obvious after studying her

from the corner of his eye. Studying her was getting to be a bit of a full-time occupation. It couldn't be helped really. And surely a woman who looked like she did would be well used to having men watching her every move? He certainly couldn't keep his eyes off her.

'Even though you've just outwitted me yet again, you mean?'

That wasn't exactly what he meant. Not that he had deliberately set out to make her look or feel silly, which would have been cruel and uncalled for, though he knew she would never let him do that without putting up a fight anyway. But he did enjoy teasing her, did enjoy proving her wrong, did enjoy the fact that their back-and-forth would reveal little bits about her personality to him, even if it maybe did end up revealing an equal amount of his along the way.

It was more to do with why she was smiling and not putting up a fight or taking offence. As if in some small way he had made progress, come up a little in her estimation. And his ego liked that.

Because he wanted—*what* exactly? For her to see that he was—what? Not a sheep farmer? Now there was a big achievement.

Nope, if he was honest with himself, it was probably that he wanted her to be smiling because she enjoyed his company, that she was allowing herself to be more comfortable around him. But why would he want that? What would be the point?

'Shouldn't you be turning your pretty little nose up about now and saying how bad it smells in here?'

Keelin smiled all the more. 'Of course it smells. But that comes with the territory, I'd expect. And nice and all as it is that you think I have a pretty nose, you've still gone right ahead and assumed that I'm some kind of porcelain doll, haven't you? Someone who's all upset at the idea of being around so many animals, who would be much happier with a glass of *Cristal* than she is with the great outdoors?'

'Aren't you?'

She stopped and looked up at him with a knowing gleam in her eyes that momentarily floored him again. How did she *do* that?

'Ooh, and now who's the one making assumptions, Mr Kincaid?'

Garrett was stunned into temporary silence. She'd got him. With a glance away from her face he shook his head, and the laughter made it up from his chest before he looked back. 'All right. You win that one.'

Keelin bowed her head. 'The wellingtons appreciate your honesty.'

'So in the absence of *Cristal* what do you want to try your hand at?'

Her chin lifted as her mouth pursed in thought. 'What are my options?'

Garrett's traitorous body suggested a few dozen options to his mind that had nothing to do with farming, though did have a choice or two linked to the great outdoors. But he ignored them and found safer ones. 'Well, this lot need to be fed before we put them out again. Or you can help herd them back into the pasture if you like, now that you're such an expert quad driver.'

'I think I can manage both of those, if you'll tell me what to do.' With a sudden, unexpected movement she reached out her hand and patted him on his back, a gleam of challenge in her eyes. 'Just you think of me as one of the boys.'

Not too likely.

Though his initial impression of her did make a distinct shift as she launched herself into each task with such enthusiasm that he ended up the one doing the smiling. What she lacked in size and physical strength she more than made up for in determination and an eagerness to try. Even though she did look entirely too cute trying it.

On which he'd lay odds she'd kick him for even thinking.

It was the expression on her face as she forked feed into the racks, as she lugged buckets from one end of the shed to the other with Garrett's dogs constantly at her heels. Her arched brows folded down in concentration, the end of her tongue often caught between her even white teeth, the flush on her cheeks.

If she was a porcelain doll then she was the new millennium's version of one. One that could look good and get down to the work when it needed to be done at the same time. A sort of super-porcelain doll.

She wiped her hands along the front of her designer jeans and tilted her head up at him as he refilled the feed bins when they were done. 'So where does the milk go from here?'

'Tankers take it to our factory at Caherciveen on the mainland. You'll have driven past it to get to the ferry.'

'You own a factory?' Her eyes widened a little in surprise. 'What do you make?'

'Organic dairy products—ice cream being one of our best-selling lines. We ship it all over the country and just recently to top-end restaurants in the UK.' He lifted another bag, tore open the top of it and poured it into the huge metal bins.

'And a hundred cows, give or take, can do all that?'

Garrett smiled. 'Nope. The girls are good but they're not that good. Most of the island's neighbours keep a herd of one size or another. Some breed them, some keep dairy herds, some raise the young males for organic meat. But there isn't that much ground here to keep them on so we have several smallholders we buy from on the mainland close by. In fact—' he folded away the last bag and clapped his hands together to remove the loose dust before he closed the lid on the bin and leaned against it '—I rarely get to spend time here on the home farm any more. I'm either at the factory or out visiting new customers, or looking for new farms that might be able to work to our codes. It's not easy converting them from the more usual methods of farming.'

It didn't take long for realization to enter her eyes. 'That's why everyone calls you boss. And why you said the island relied on you being more than—'

'Just a sheep farmer?'

A tinge of pink crept up over her cheeks and he chuckled in response, which brought an answering smile to her lips. 'You could have just told me that.'

'Yes, I could. But then I'd have missed out on—'

Keelin placed a hand on her hip, tilting her head in challenge. 'Making me feel like a *complete* idiot?'

The easier answer would have been to get to spend time on the home farm, which he genuinely missed on the days when he was loaded down with paperwork, or research development, or away on one of his business trips. But that wouldn't be the truth. Not the bigger truth anyway.

He would have missed out on getting to spend more time in her company without making it obvious to either of them that that was what he was doing.

Thing was, now that he *had* spent more time in her company, since he'd had a glimpse into the person she was, and the difficulties she was having with her own life, he couldn't bring himself to lie to her, not completely.

'Maybe I just wanted to take the opportunity to impress you a little.' Which wasn't a lie. 'Even if you did set yourself up rightly for a target in the looking-like-an-idiot department. You came across as a bit of a snob, you have to admit.'

'Only because you have such a talent for bringing out the worst in me.'

'If I do, it's unintentional.'

'Is it?' Her brows arched in challenge. 'This from the man who basically told me to butt out and keep my distance the first night I was here. You can't blame a girl for being defensive after that, you know.'

Garrett pushed off the edge of the bin and towered over her, a frown on his face. 'And yet that same man felt the need to hug you within an hour of meeting you.'

Keelin stared up at him for a long, long time.

And Garrett couldn't read the thoughts as they crossed her eyes, because he was mesmerized by how her pupils had enlarged, how the usual vibrant blue had taken on a deeper, almost cobalt shade, and then his gaze dropped and followed the swipe of her tongue over her mouth.

He bunched his hands into fists by his sides, determined that he wouldn't make the mistake of reaching for her again. As if by even mentioning it aloud he had converted it into some kind of deep-seated need.

They weren't arguing. Their words had been softly, almost calmly spoken. But then they couldn't really make them into angry accusations, could they? Not when they were the truth.

But there was still enough tension in the air, enough simmering beneath the surface.

And Garrett knew he wasn't the only one that felt that when Keelin's voice came out with a huskier edge than normal.

'That was instinctual, was all. You were offering sympathy to a weeping woman.' She managed a small smile. 'It was actually very gentlemanly of you.'

'You needed someone to hold you for a minute.'

Her eyes shone, but she blinked hard, covering up the flash of remembered emotion with a small burst of almost nervous laughter. 'Well, it was nice of you. But, now that you know me a little better, I hope you know I'm capable of looking after myself. Even if I don't put that across very well sometimes.'

The words were out before he could stop them. 'No one should have to go it alone, Keelin.'

'You do.' Her chin rose. 'You haven't married since Terri's mother died. And that had to have been your choice. I doubt very much that on a place as small as this one you weren't inundated with offers from single women.'

Ignoring the half-compliment in her words, Garrett tore his gaze from hers and examined his feet for a brief second while he battled with his inner self on the subject of leaving her be, or pushing her on the things he wanted to know.

When he looked back up, the intensity in her gaze made the decision for him. 'I'm not on my own like you are, though, am I? I have Terri and Dermot; we're a family. What does Keelin O'Donnell have waiting for her out there?'

He hadn't asked if there was a boyfriend, or a lover, or a combination of the two that was more serious. He didn't have to, because the intimation was already there. And if he'd taken the time to be harder on himself he'd have thought it might have been less obvious he was fishing if he hadn't just spelled it out. And asked her if she fancied staying longer on the island to see if she could consider seeing what was possible. *With him.*

It wasn't as if the attraction weren't already there. Leastways not on his part. But what was he—seventeen all over again? Keen to make a fool of himself, again?

'What difference does it make to you who's there for me, Garrett?' She tried to ease the words with another small smile. 'It's not like I'm going to call you up and ask for a hug when I'm hundreds of miles away.'

Garrett glanced away and shrugged his shoulders. 'Like I said, I just don't think anyone should have to go it alone. Not someone who has already said they'd like the chance to be happy.'

'Like you are?'

The words stung. That was just the thing, wasn't it? He had his family, his successful business, the respect of the islanders and the people he dealt with on a daily basis. But was he happy?

Garrett wasn't so sure he could say that, especially now he'd experienced the exhilaration he'd felt of late in Keelin's company. Instead he looked at her from the corner of his eye and smiled a slow smile. 'I'd like the chance to be. Just like everyone else.'

Keelin stared up at him with wide, unblinking eyes. And for a split second Garrett almost moved towards her, the invisible cord pulling him in again, tugging so hard that he really couldn't fight it.

'There you are. I wondered what was keeping you.'

They both turned to look at Dermot where he stood at the other end of the large shed. He smiled down at them, then waved an arm in invitation.

'Bring Keelin into the house for some tea, Garrett. You've had her slaving out here long enough. And you can't do anything more here 'til this lot have finished eating.'

'We were just coming in.' Garrett smiled back at him, before waiting for Keelin to start walking at his side.

Close to the end of the barn and Dermot's waiting figure, with his head bowed as he matched his longer stride to her pace, Garrett heard her voice sound low beside him.

'You didn't have to try and impress me with what you do for a living, Garrett. The kind of man you are already did that.'

CHAPTER NINE

'CAN I get wellingtons like Keelin's, Dad?'

Keelin laughed as Garrett rolled his eyes. It felt good to be back inside the fold of his family again, even briefly, and even if she now knew without a shadow of a doubt that there wasn't a place in it that belonged to her. Not that they were treating her any differently this time than they had the night she had come to dinner.

Except that this time Garrett wasn't frowning at her; in fact if anything he was avoiding looking at her directly in front of everyone else.

And Keelin knew that was because of the conversation they had had before Dermot had interrupted them...

The conversation that had reached a pause, where Keelin had never wanted so badly to be kissed and yet been so afraid of being kissed at the same time.

But he hadn't kissed her, which was maybe just as well. Somehow she knew, deep inside where a woman just *knew*, that he was exactly the kind of man who would kiss a woman clean off her feet. Whose kiss would place a brand on her that could never be removed. And how could Keelin walk away with that imprint on her? When walking away was exactly what she knew she had to do.

She'd already done enough damage by telling him he impressed her.

'Do they do ones with butterflies on?'

Garrett pointed a long finger across the table. 'You answer that and you're in trouble.'

'I can't answer that, apparently, Terri.' Keelin leaned forwards, her eyes sparkling as she dropped her voice to a stage whisper. 'But I *do* know you can get them with sequins and glitter on…'

Garrett groaned.

And Terri giggled as she came up behind him, wrapping her arms around his neck and resting her chin on his shoulder. 'They could be special occasions wellies. Christmas, Easter, birthdays, that kind of thing. You'd barely notice they were there.'

'They'd be hard to miss.' His hand rose from the table top, settling on Terri's smaller joined hands at the base of his throat as he turned his face towards her. 'Even from space. Wouldn't you prefer a nice navy pair? Or green?'

'You're so-o boring, Dad. Don't be an old stuck-in-the-mud.'

'There's a joke in there about wellingtons and being stuck in the mud.'

'Ha, ha.' Terri's eyes were sparkling with amusement as she looked across the table at Keelin. 'Help me out here, Keelin. We can't have him being so unadventurous his whole life, can we?'

Garrett's eyes locked with Keelin's across the table and she swallowed hard. If answering Terri's earlier question would have got her into trouble, then how *could* she have answered this one…?

Keelin silently cleared her throat. 'Having seen your dad on a quad I don't think unadventurous really fits him.'

'I bet *you've* had loads of cool adventures.'

Her mouth curved into an easier smile. 'Not any I could tell you about. I might put ideas in your head.'

And the warmth in Garrett's eyes made her smile all the

more. Because he really wanted to know what it was she had done before or because he was grateful she hadn't encouraged Terri to run off somewhere by making it sound 'fun'? Keelin decided she could accept either answer and be happy. Even if either of them could be translated as her hoping he was impressed by *her*.

Thing was, she really hadn't done anything to impress him so far, had she? And even though that shouldn't have mattered any more to Keelin than it probably did to Garrett, it was there nevertheless. It was a need as real to her as thirst, or hunger.

But then surely it was only natural when being so very aware of someone, so *very* attracted to them, that she would want him to feel the same way back. No matter how pointless that might be in the long term.

'And what did your mother think of your adventures?'

She turned to look at Dermot, whose eyes flickered from her to Garrett and back again, just briefly. But long enough for Keelin to have noticed it, and for her to wonder just how much he was seeing.

'That was just the thing. I think I tried some of my wilder adventures to get her attention and all she did was shrug them off and say that I'd find my own boundaries in time. That I'd see sense as I got older because the only one it really reflected on was me.'

Dermot nodded. 'Yes, that sounds like your mother all right. She'd have understood someone's need to express their freedom. And she'd lived enough herself to know when to stand back and when to intervene.'

'She never intervened. I think that's why I stopped in the end; it wasn't getting me the attention I thought it would.'

Another nod, this time accompanied by a small smile. 'Well, you mustn't have done anything too awful, then. Or she'd have stopped you.'

'*Did* you do anything that awful?'

Her gaze was brought back to Garrett's face as he asked the question. 'Nothing that I thought would do me harm, no. But the odd reckless thing, yes.'

'Oh-h-h, now I really wanna know what you did!'

Keelin laughed at Terri's expression. 'Find your own adventures! I won't get the blame that way.'

'Fat chance of that—' Terri untangled herself from her father's shoulders and stepped back '—when I'm not even allowed adventurous *wellies*.'

Garrett's gaze dropped to the large mug he held cradled in his large hands. And even though Keelin couldn't hear him sigh, she saw how his wide chest rose and fell beneath his dark navy sweater. With his thick lashes hiding the warmth in his eyes from her, she couldn't search them for anger at either Terri's words, or the words Keelin had spoken that let her voice her objection in the first place. But somehow she could sense the resignation in him. As if this was a much bigger battle that had been ongoing for a long time before she had arrived, and would probably continue long after she was gone.

She'd never had to look at it closely from a parent's point of view. But with their brief chat about her mother's method of dealing with Keelin's need for adventure still ringing in her mind, she could see that there was no right and wrong.

So, feeling a little braver with Garrett than she had before, she took a chance. 'Maybe you and your dad could come up with some adventures to take together. That could be fun, right?'

Terri studied the back of her father's head for a long moment, before looking at Keelin with an expression that almost begged for help.

Well, in for a penny. 'You could both talk over some ideas of things you'd like to do or places you'd like to go. There'd be nearly as much fun in the planning of it, don't you think?'

Terri shrugged. 'Maybe. Depends what we'd be doing.'

'Well, why don't you try thinking up a few ideas and running them past your dad?'

With her focus on the flash of hope in Terri's eyes, she felt rather than saw Garrett's eyes on her. But now that there was a window of opportunity, and she'd flung it open without thought of repercussion, Keelin wasn't quite ready to look at him and have her great idea shot down by his anger at her interference.

So she took a breath. 'What would you like to do?'

There was only the briefest of hesitation. 'I'd really like to go shopping in Dublin. But that's a girl thing and Dad would hate that.'

And there wasn't a mother-figure or even an aunt or grand-mother to take her, was there? Keelin's heart twisted in her chest at the thought.

This time she did look at Garrett, searching the toffee eyes she now knew so well for a sign of him thinking the same thing. His thick lashes flickered a barely perceptible amount as he met her searching gaze. His sensual mouth parted as if he might say something, but no words came. So Keelin dragged her gaze away and smiled up at Terri.

'Well, if you clear it with your dad, I could take you shopping. But you have to promise me that you'll both make some plans of things you can do together—a concert or a weekend sightseeing maybe?' She was on a roll now, warming to her subject as she leaned a little more over the table. 'It doesn't even have to be Dublin; you could go further afield. And make it something you do regularly—maybe a few times a year. You think you can do that?'

Terri looked as if all her Christmases had arrived at once. 'Really, you'll take me shopping?'

It hadn't had quite the effect that she'd been looking for.

And Keelin's enthusiasm waned slightly as she sat back again in her chair. She was trying to get Terri to spend time with her father, not ingratiate herself because she didn't mind going shopping. Which was any man's worst nightmare. But if one bribe from Keelin could bring about a pact between father and daughter about other trips they could take *together?*

'If it's okay with your dad.' She looked at Garrett again, lifting her eyebrows in question when she was met with only an intense stare.

Please, Garrett. I'm trying here.

Dermot leaned forwards on the table and added his two cent's worth. 'If it gets you out of a day wandering around women's shops then I'd jump at it in your shoes.'

The room practically held its breath. Until, finally, Garrett took a breath and a smile started in his eyes before it made it to his mouth; a wry smile, the kind of smile that was magnanimous in defeat.

'Why do I get the feeling I'm being ganged up on here?'

Keelin nodded, her mouth pursed into a fine line for a second before she smiled back at him. 'Because you are. Nothing stands between girls and shopping. Not without one heck of a fight.'

'Please, Dad?' Terri's arms were around his neck again as she pleaded into his ear. 'Please, please, pretty please?'

'Not Dublin, it's too far away—'

'But, Dad—'

He lifted a hand to her arm again and turned his face towards her. 'Killarney is closer. You can't ask Keelin to drive all the way to Dublin and back.'

'But, *Dad*—'

Keelin grasped at the middle ground. 'Shopping is shopping, honey. And I've not shopped in Killarney so it'll be as much fun for me as it is for you. We can go early, shop, have a nice lunch somewhere glam and then shop some more. If your dad is a good boy we might even bring him back something…'

Garrett looked briefly at her and then back at Terri with a nod. 'See? Everyone's happy. Though maybe you should be the one to tell her that the words Killarney and glam don't get used in the same sentence too much round here.'

Terri squeezed his neck so hard that she would probably have choked a lesser man. Then she kissed his cheek and ran round the table, completely stunning Keelin when she hugged and kissed her the same way.

'Thank you so much. You're terrific! I've never got to do a real girlie day shopping and I've always wanted to.'

So much information in one small sentence. And Keelin was unbelievably touched by the open affection, given so freely and so easily. How could a mother ever have taken a chance on leaving her behind, this child who had so much to give? And who needed a mother more now than she ever had, as she took the first tentative steps towards womanhood.

It was so very unfair.

And a sudden memory entered Keelin's mind, of when her own mother had taken her on her first 'grown-up' shopping trip, when they had spent a day trawling through Paris, spending ridiculous amounts of money and drinking hot chocolate in bistros. And talking, and laughing.

How had she forgotten that?

Without knowing it Terri had given Keelin a massive gift in return for a much smaller gift.

'I'd better go put the herd out; I let the lads go early for Sunday lunch seeing I'm here.'

It took Keelin a second to focus her mind back on the present, so enthralled was she by the unexpected gift of a precious memory from the past. She watched Garrett push back from the table, watched him avoid looking at her or Terri, so with a smile and a returning hug for her new-found best friend she extricated herself and pushed back her own chair.

'Another chance to play on a quad—I can't miss that, now, can I?'

Dermot smiled up at her, his eyes gleaming. 'No, can't have you miss that. I'm sure Garrett will be glad of the help and the company...'

Keelin's eyes widened. *Uh-oh.*

But Dermot merely chuckled. 'Just make sure you two are in for lunch by three.'

'We always have Sunday lunch later.' Terri sidled past her, leaning her head closer to add. 'It's so these two old fogies can laze around and watch sports for the afternoon.'

'You really don't have to go to the bother of lunch for me, Dermot. I only came to learn a bit about farming because it's something I've never done and—' She was babbling, wasn't she? Oh, terrific. She was babbling and Dermot was looking at her with a gleam in his eyes that said he knew she was babbling.

'Nonsense, child. You put in a morning's work here the least we can do is feed you.' Dermot glanced over at Garrett. 'She looks like she could do with a feeding too, don't you think, Garrett?'

He had just handed Garrett an open invitation to look her down and up. Which he did. *Slowly.* And everywhere he looked seemed to warm and tingle as if he had actually touched her there, until once again his gaze locked with hers and the blazing heat in that gaze almost knocked her back a step onto her heels. Oh, Lord. If he could do that with a look, then, if ever he kissed her...

She'd never survive.

Garrett looked sideways at Dermot for a brief second, his eyes seeming to narrow the tiniest little bit, then he looked back at Keelin and finally answered in a gruff. 'You may as well say yes, 'cos he's not going to let it drop 'til you do. He can be stubborn that way.'

Keelin pinned a smile on her face and nodded at Dermot. 'Runs in the family, I know. Well, all right, then, thank you.'

Garrett sighed heavily, just as he had when he had known he was beaten a few minutes ago, stepping towards and past her, his upper arm unintentionally touching her shoulder. 'You better go get the flowery wellingtons on then…'

He was waiting outside, pacing up and down the narrow pathway with his head bowed, when she made it outside.

'Sorry, Dermot was asking me what I did and didn't eat. I didn't mean to keep you.'

His head rose, fringe flopping across his forehead as he looked at her from beneath his thick lashes. Then his head turned, giving her a view of his profile, his strong jaw-line working for a second as if he was wrestling with something. And then he looked back at her.

'You didn't have to do that, you know.'

'Tell Dermot what I did or didn't eat?' She tried smiling to ease the sudden tension, teasing him even though she was fully aware what he meant. 'I might have a nut allergy and he could kill me. You wouldn't let me do that to his poor conscience, would you?'

'That's not what I meant.'

Keelin nodded, her voice soft. 'I know.'

'I could have taken her.' He shrugged. 'I've taken her shopping before.'

'Not the quite the same thing, though, is it?'

'No.' There was a minute burst of self-deprecating laughter. 'No, it's not.'

Keelin continued smiling, even while she felt a warm flush growing at the base of her neck. 'It's only one day, Garrett, and I'll enjoy it. It's not that big a deal.'

Dark brows folded down into a frown. 'It is to her.'

The flush grew in intensity and headed rapidly upwards

towards her cheeks as she realized Garrett stood on the edge of misunderstanding. Keelin couldn't have him thinking that she didn't get what it meant; she just didn't need him feeling he was beholden to her in some way either.

'I know it is. But you don't need to thank me.' She raised her chin as she walked down the path. 'It's a day's shopping, is all, it's not like I'm donating a kidney, so you don't need to make it into more of a big deal than it is, really you don't. Forget about it.'

She was almost past him when his arm shot out and his hand grasped hers, long fingers threading with slender as he tilted his head down a little to tell her in a husky voice, 'Don't hide behind jokes with me, Keelin. I wasn't just thanking you for the shopping trip. I know what you were trying to do in there.'

Keelin swallowed hard to dislodge the large lump in her throat as his thumb brushed back and forth against the fleshy skin at the base of hers. 'It's no big deal.'

She could feel his eyes studying the top of her head, his voice sounding closer. 'Actually it's more of a *big deal* than you could possibly know. And even without knowing that you still did something to try and help. When I was such an ass to you the last time you tried befriending her.'

Turning and lifting her head, she looked up into his eyes, squeezing his fingers in reassurance. 'She's just growing up, Garrett, that's all. She's going through things, that, no matter how you want to understand them, you won't be able to. Because you're a man and she's a young woman. You need time to get to know her as a young woman—' she shrugged it off and untangled her hand from his warm hold, stepping back into a safer place, where she wouldn't be so aware of him again: his breathing, his scent, his very size and strength '—and a way to do that kinda came to me, that's all. It seemed like a good idea.'

'It was. And one I should have thought of myself.'

'Sometimes the most obvious solution is what it takes us the longest to find.' She stopped a little down the path from him and turned around to study his back. She wished she had the right to step forwards and offer comfort to him, to hold him just for the sake of it. Because it was simply, the one thing he needed most.

Just as he had for her when she had needed it the day she'd arrived.

But she couldn't. Not with Garrett. It would be too much. If she held onto him then she might not want to let go and she could hardly expect one person to solve all the other things she had to sort out in her life.

The timing was wrong, that was all. It just wasn't the right time in her life to fall in love.

He turned around and marched down the path on long, confident strides, a calm smile on his face as he walked by her. 'Let's go get these beasts out, then.'

CHAPTER TEN

IT HAPPENED so quickly. And yet played out in slow motion across his optical nerves, and probably would for a very long time afterwards.

They'd barely spoken since they'd got back onto the quads, barring the exchange of instructions needed for following the meandering herd back out onto the allocated pasture. And Garrett was grateful for that.

Because for the first time in his life he really couldn't think of anything else to say. Keelin had done one hell of a number on him really. Not content with having distracted him from day one, or having gradually started to crawl in under his skin, she was now, without even knowing how big a deal it was, mending bridges between him and the most important person in his life.

How did she *do* that?

And not just that. He had seen the look on her face when Terri had hugged her, when it was as if a light switched on inside her and she glowed under the warmth of such a small show of affection.

And in that moment Garrett had wanted that look to stay on her face. He had looked over at the two of them in each other's arms and his heart had crumpled into a tight ball inside his chest.

There was no way in hell he was talking about *that*.

Instead he had focused all his attention on the herd, glad of the odd stray that kept him on his toes so he didn't have time to think, or do anything beyond glance at Keelin to see where she was and that she was doing okay.

But it was that focus to remain on safe ground, mentally, that led him to miss Keelin taking off after a stray on her own. He didn't notice until it was already too late and the animal took off at the run, with Keelin trying to round it back.

'Keelin, leave it!'

He wasn't sure she could hear him across the field and above the sound of the quad engine, but he could feel the bubble of fear in his chest, so he tried anyway.

'Keelin!'

It happened so quickly.

One minute she was chasing the cow, then it veered and she veered with it. But the quad hit a rut and bounced, and she bounced out of the side and hit the ground.

And Garrett's heart stopped.

It seemed to take for ever for him to get across the field. By then he could already see her moving, so the thundering in his ears eased and the bubble in his chest changed from fear into anger as he reached her side.

'What the *hell* did you think you were doing?'

Sitting up, she stared at him with wide eyes in a pale face. 'That's right, go ahead and yell at me, 'cos I'm fine, *really*, thanks for asking.'

He turned off the engine and swung a leg to dismount, then he was kneeling beside her, his eyes taking in the mud all over her designer jeans, the one flowery wellington half off her foot, the grass stain on one of her cheeks, the mussed-up hair that had broken free from her single plait.

She was beautiful even when she was messy.

'Do you hurt anywhere?'

'Apart from my pride, you mean?'

'Right this second I don't actually give a damn about your pride; I'm more concerned about broken bones.'

'I haven't broken anything.'

But he was already reaching out and feeling up her leg from her ankle, his large hands gentle, yet firm as they searched for injuries. And he tried his best not to react to the fact he had a reason to touch her openly, an excuse to touch her even though she would have been screaming in pain if something really *was* broken…

As she moved round a little on her backside Keelin's small hand slapped his away. 'Stop that; I'm fine!'

'I need to check—'

'The hell you do.' She slapped his hands away again. 'Seriously, stop that. I can tell you if I hurt anywhere, I'm not *unconscious!*'

He scowled hard as he looked up into her wide eyes. What he saw there temporarily rocked him back on his heels. His gaze dropped lower, to her parted lips, to the pulse beating in the base of her neck, to the rise and fall of her breasts as she took shaky breaths.

But Garrett knew instinctively it wasn't just shock from the fall. With his hands still on her calf, he spread his fingers wide, circling her leg, moving his fingertips up to the sensitive area behind her knee.

And she gasped.

His voice dropped. 'Does that hurt?'

Keelin damped her lips as she looked down at her knee. 'No.'

Lifting his hands to her other leg, but with his gaze fixed on her face, he repeated the process—hands sliding up her calf, fingers spreading, moving his fingertips up to the sensitive area behind her knee. And was rewarded with another, albeit better disguised, gasp, which made him smile a small, very intimate smile.

'That?'

She knew he knew. He could tell it from the way her eyes narrowed and the flush grew on her cheeks. But if he hadn't got it from that he would have from the way she once again slapped his hands away, sidling backwards on her rear.

'All right, that's enough. I'm *fine* and I think we *both* know I am.'

Garrett chuckled. And Keelin glared at him.

So he pushed upwards, holding out a hand for her; a hand that she ignored as she tried as gracefully as possible to get to her feet.

She almost managed it too, until she tried putting weight on her left ankle and it gave under her.

Garrett reached out and caught her arms as she yelped. 'Okay. Not so fine after all, then.'

'I must have twisted it. It's not broken.'

'Well, *Dr O'Donnell,* much as I value that opinion, how about we get an actual professional to look at it?' He adjusted an arm. 'Put your arm around my waist and lean on me.'

There was a moment of hesitation.

'Keelin. All I'm doing is helping you take the weight off that ankle.'

She looked up at him from the corner of her eye, having to take a moment to blow a strand of hair out of her face. And Garrett chuckled again at the look of suspicion on her face.

But the glare she gave him forced him to control himself. So he stepped back and held his hands up, palms towards her as he shrugged. 'Go right ahead, then; I'll go rescue your quad.'

It had stalled after she'd fallen off, and was sitting at an angle in the end of the long rut. But even as he bounced it up onto even ground he was watching Keelin from the corner of his eye. She really was being stubborn to the point of stupidity.

Was the idea of leaning on someone, even for so practical a reason, just too much for her? Or was the fact that she now knew he was as physically aware of her as he now knew she was of him just too much and entirely too soon? It should have been in his own mind, if he had any sense left at all...

But the only thing in his mind was what had just happened and his responsibility for it. What in hell had he been thinking? It was almost as if he had set her a range of challenges and sat back waiting for her to fail so that he could prove to himself that she didn't and never could fit into a place like this.

And she'd risen to every challenge, hadn't she? Despite her ridiculous wellingtons, her designer clothes and her fragile beauty.

The very fragility that could have been irreparably broken with a bad fall off the lump of machinery he was now turning around to face her limping figure.

What did he want from her?

Setting her challenges was pointless. It wouldn't change the life she already had or the fact that inevitably she would go back to it.

'Where exactly is it you think you're going?' Some of the frustration at himself came through in his voice as he glared over at her.

Already frowning through the pain from her ankle, Keelin lifted her head before she answered in a tight voice. 'Determined and all as I am, I doubt I can make it back to the house without getting back on the quad. I know my limits.'

'Oh-h-h, you're not getting back on the quad.'

'Then what do you expect me to do?'

Angrily tugging the key from her quad, he pushed it deep into the pocket of his jeans before striding towards her with a determined stare. Keelin's eyes widened, she even hopped back a step from him before he got to her.

And swept her up into his arms.

'*Garrett!*' His name came out on a shriek of surprise. 'Put me down!'

'I'll put you down when you're back in the house.'

She struggled in his arms. 'I mean it: *put me down*. I can get back to the house on the quad.'

'Not with that ankle, you can't. You won't be able to use your foot to change gears.' He hoisted her up in his arms and held her tighter, feeling her arm grip around his neck before she struggled again. 'Fight all you want, Keelin; I'm carrying you back.'

'You're going to march all the way across this field and up the lane *carrying me?* It's *miles* away! This is ridiculous.'

Garrett kept marching on in determined strides. 'Yeah, 'cos you weigh so much it's going to take all that much effort. And it's not miles; it's a bit of a stretch of the legs, that's all.'

The sarcasm made her struggle again. 'Then take me on *your* quad. I've never had anyone carry me my entire life.'

'As long as you're within my sight you're never getting on a quad again.'

She stopped struggling. And he kept marching.

'You can't seriously be blaming yourself for me falling off?'

His shoulders dropped a little.

And Keelin knew straight away that that was exactly what he was doing. He was used to taking on responsibility after all—that was what he did; responsibility for family, for the daughter who had been left by her mother, for half the island's income. But *this* hadn't been his fault; *she* wasn't his responsibility,

'They're called accidents for a reason, you know.'

Even the softening of her voice had no effect. Instead he kept walking across the field, his jaw tight, his gaze determined and fixed on his destination.

So Keelin sighed and tried again. 'How is it your fault? I turned too tight and hit a bump, that's all.'

'You wouldn't have been on it in the first place if it wasn't for me.'

'*Oh, for goodness' sake!*' She attempted another struggle to get free but it was futile. Not only was she in a position that didn't allow her much movement, she also had the fact that every time she moved her legs there was a sharp pain from her ankle up into her calf—and then there was the more obvious, much more sensual barrier.

Garrett was carrying her as if she weighed nothing. And Keelin knew that wasn't just down to dress size. He was just so strong, the chest against which she was held was so broad and tight, the arms that held her two bands of steel.

Never in her life had she been so aware of someone else's *body*, and maybe she should have just known she would be seriously affected by being so close to it after all their earlier encounters. The warning signs had certainly been there. But then she hadn't lied to him either; it *was* the first time any man had picked her up and carried her.

It was the sexiest, most romantic thing ever.

But it was also the most terrifying. Because with it came a sudden sense of realization.

This just couldn't happen this fast! It had only been a few days! People just didn't feel this aware, this attracted, this emotionally attached to someone in that short a space of time.

Was she so desperate for someone to care about her? So lonely? So afraid of being on her own that she would let herself fixate on the first gorgeous male she met?

Or was it simply that the romance of the letters had been influencing her before she'd even got here?

She struggled again.

'You might not weigh that much, but all the struggling isn't making this any easier. Stay still or I'll drop you on purpose.'

Keelin wasn't sure that wouldn't be the better option. But even as she opened her mouth to say as much he hoisted her up again, so that she was forced to cling tighter to him. To raise her free hand to join the one that was already wrapped around the strong column of his neck, so that her fingers were brushing against coarse hair, cushioned against his heated skin.

Garrett kept walking; Keelin stayed still—well aware she had no choice but to submit to being carried. And just in case it never happened again in her lifetime, she allowed herself to enjoy the moment. To store it away in her memory with every-thing else she knew she would never forget about him.

But eventually she felt she had to say *something*.

'So does this mean I have to report in to you every time I do something vaguely risky from now on? Even after I leave? Now that you've taken on sole responsibility for my welfare and all.'

'Nope, once you leave you're on your own.'

Her breath caught in her chest at the words.

And immediately his chest rose and fell as he took a deep breath, his arms tightening for a brief moment. 'I'm sorry, I shouldn't have said that.'

'You can't help it when it's true.'

'You have to have friends, though—you're not completely alone?'

'Yes, I have friends. They're a bit spread out, though. But I guess at least that way I always have somewhere to visit. And I'm a godmother to three gorgeous kids now too so I have a good excuse to visit.'

'But no family of your own.'

'Not any more.' She tilted her chin so she could look up at him and was rewarded when he looked down at her with his warm toffee eyes. 'There should really be violins playing some-where, don't you think?'

Garrett didn't smile. 'There you go making jokes again to cover up the bigger stuff.'

'Well, there's not much I can do about it; that's just the way it is. Everyone has something to deal with. And I still have a few years left in me to start a family of my own.'

His voice dropped an octave. 'And is that what you want?'

Keelin tried her best not to answer him too honestly. It wasn't something she had planned on doing for a few years, but then it wasn't as if she had that many candidates to help her out; not solid, grounded ones with the kind of irresistible intensity she found in Garrett. If there had been…

But Garrett's world was a universe away from hers and Keelin had responsibilities now. She had a legacy to oversee, a life to plan for herself, a place to find that she could call home. She had to keep reminding herself of that, especially now.

Falling for Garrett wouldn't change any of those things.

'One day maybe. I have a fair bit to do before then.'

'Like what?'

She smiled. 'You don't really want to know.'

Garrett quirked a brow in response. 'I wouldn't have asked if I didn't want to know. Surely you've got that about me by now?'

Yes, she had. Amongst many, *many* other things.

'Maybe I'd prefer you not to think of me as some pathetic little figure any more than you already do.'

'I don't think of you as some pathetic little figure. You have to have got that by now, too.'

His voice and the excruciating warmth in his eyes almost crushed her. And yet, even when she should have left it alone for safety's sake, she still allowed herself to ask. 'And what way *do* you think of me?'

'I don't know that you really want to hear that right now.'

'I wouldn't have asked if I didn't want to know. Surely you've got that about me by now?'

Garrett smiled a full-blown, dimpled smile. 'You have a smart mouth, Miss O'Donnell.'

'Well, that's one thing you think of me. Keep going now you've got started; I can take it.'

He shook his head, then chuckled, the sound reverberating in his chest so that it vibrated against Keelin's breasts and set her pulse flurrying.

'You're not as fragile as you look on the outside.'

'And yet here I am being carried across the hills and dales…'

'Hating every minute of it 'cos you'd rather fight your own battles, even while injured…'

Keelin stared up at him for a long moment, then confessed in a low voice. 'Not actually hating it right this minute, if you must know. It's one of those things I guess every woman would like to have happen to them at some stage. So I'm just going to irritate you by enjoying it and that'll make me feel much better about what it's doing to my reputation for being capable.' And she rested her cheek against his collar-bone, her forehead against his jaw. 'Keep going.'

He took another deep breath that lifted her head for a second. 'You're beautiful. But you knew that already.'

Keelin smiled, silently sighing as she nestled closer. 'My mother said in one of her letters that beauty is just an outer thing; it fades with time. What's inside matters more and that's why everybody should strive to be beautiful as a person.'

'She was a very wise woman.'

'It was something Dermot told to her when she was here. And he told her that was what she was to him and always would be. Beautiful inside and out.'

Garrett leaned his head back a little so he could see Keelin's face. 'Dermot said that?'

When Keelin looked up she smiled at the look of incredulity on his face. 'He was young once too you know.'

'Yeah, but who'd have known he was such a romantic?' Garrett grinned. 'Any wonder my mother adored him 'til the day she died. Go Dermot!'

Keelin laughed. 'You could learn something from him.'

'I'm carrying you across a field, isn't that chivalrous enough for you?'

'W-e-l-l...' She tilted her head from side to side, then yelped in surprise when he hoisted her upwards again.

'Careful now. I really might drop you.'

Keelin pouted. 'You wouldn't drop me.'

A gleam of sheer mischief entered his eyes and Keelin felt shiver of anticipation. But whatever she could have anticipated didn't prepare her for him suddenly dropping her a couple of feet, then catching her before hoisting her up again, changing position and swinging her over his shoulder.

With her head swinging upside down and her hair everywhere as it came loose, she felt his laughter through her stomach as she yelled at him, laughing herself. 'All right, all right, you've made your point. I take it back. The way you were carrying me before was *very* chivalrous. *And romantic.*'

'I didn't hear that.'

She thumped a small fist off his broad back. 'Yes, you did! Garrett, put me back!'

'Say please.'

'*Please!*' She giggled uncontrollably, despite her situation. The blood is rushing to my head!'

He stopped walking. And with agonizing slowness he allowed her body to slide down along the length of his until her head came back over his shoulder and she slid low enough that her face was level with his. Where she smiled at him, despite the rush of heat over her body, the pounding of her heart against her ribcage and the sudden sense of dizziness she knew she couldn't totally credit to having been upside down.

With his nose almost touching hers, and his warm breath fanning her lips, he smiled back. 'I think you take defeat quite well; 's a sign that you're a good sport. Men like that in a woman.'

Keelin stared at him, then nodded slowly. 'You know, I'm even starting to like me a little from this description.'

'And so you should. You're an amazing woman.'

She could barely breathe, the air around them seeming to crackle with the intensity of the moment. 'Thank you.'

Garrett's smile faded a little as he lowered her carefully to the ground. 'You're welcome.'

Balancing more on her good foot than her bad, Keelin looked up at him, silently willing him to kiss her. Just the one time, *please.* Just once so she could know what it was like to be knocked clean off her feet, to be so thoroughly kissed that she was branded with his touch long after she'd left. So she would never forget or settle for less.

But the warmth in his eyes had already faded. He looked over her shoulder towards the laneway, then leaned down and swept her back up into his arms again. So that she was once again left looking at his jaw-line from her nestled position against his shoulder.

What was wrong? She had been so sure this time. And so very ready to be kissed by him.

He started walking again, and was silent for several steps onto the lane before he asked in a low, husky voice, 'Why do you think she still left him in the end?'

It took Keelin a long moment to unscramble her thoughts enough to get his meaning. 'You mean my mother?'

'Yes.' He took another breath, every step bringing them closer to the house. 'Why would she leave him if they were so in love?'

'I don't know. I haven't got to that part yet.'

Garrett tilted his head back to look down at her face. 'Let me know when you do.'

'I will.' And she knew she would, because she needed so badly to know herself. Leaving this place had to have been one of the most difficult things her mother had ever done. And Keelin knew that so clearly. *Now.*

Because leaving it was going to kill a part of *Keelin,* wasn't it?

CHAPTER ELEVEN

THE doctor declared that her ankle was, as Keelin had already predicted, *not* broken. But even so Dermot wouldn't let her return to the hotel, under *any* circumstances.

No matter how much Keelin protested while Garrett remained silent.

The silent brooding continued for much of the rest of the day when he was inside the house and not off outside doing farm stuff. Oh, he talked when he needed to, joined in the conversation at lunch, showed enthusiasm while Terri excitedly came up with different ideas for things they could do together.

But it wasn't the same.

And Keelin ached for the loss of his warm gaze and the teasing light in his eyes, for the tentative friendship they had built up since their 'new beginnings' handshake in the bar the night before.

When she should maybe have welcomed the chance to take in some air and calm her thoughts. To rein in the feelings she didn't seem to have any control over when he was close to her.

Most of all to slow down the runaway train of emotions she had around him. She had to find a way to do that most of all. Because it had only been a few days, and yet she felt as if she'd lived a lifetime in them.

As if some things had changed in her that she couldn't change back.

One of those things being how much of a feeling of warmth and belonging she felt inside a family environment. The constant background noise of television or radio and *constantly* the voices and movement of others, the latter of which offered a sense of comfort she had never really experienced. It meant that even when she was silent she wasn't aware of silence, or of any sense of loneliness. Because she knew she wasn't alone. They were all there.

She could just lie back on the sofa she'd been allocated, Garrett's dogs at her side, and watch them all. And experience for a while a taster of what her life could be like some day.

Keelin couldn't ever remember her soul being more at peace.

'I've made you up a room, Keelin, but I'm afraid you'll have to make it upstairs.' Dermot smiled ruefully at her a few hours after Terri had gone to bed and Garrett had come in from the animals. 'Do you think you can manage?'

'I'll take her up.'

Keelin's gaze shot in Garrett's direction, a slither of anticipation running down her spine at the thought of being carried again. But as she glanced back at Dermot's studious eyes examining Garrett's impassive face, she knew it would be much safer to find a way of hopping up the stairs on her own.

The look on both Terri's and his faces when Garrett and Keelin had returned had already told a tale. And she couldn't let them believe it meant something more, especially Terri, who had worn a look of hope that had almost crushed Keelin.

'I can make it.'

Garrett blinked calmly at her. 'The Doctor said you were to keep your weight off it for at least twenty-four hours.'

Keelin tilted her head and smirked. 'You think I can't hop on my good leg? Little old independent me? I'll make it. I'll shimmy up on my backside if I have to.'

From the corner of her eye she saw Dermot silently watching the brief interplay. How could Garrett not notice it too? And why would he let it continue knowing what thoughts his step-father might have been having?

As if he'd read her mind, he glanced at Dermot from the corner of his eye, and shrugged, pushing up off his armchair and lifting his empty tea-mug. 'Fine, then.'

He patted his thigh for the dogs to follow him, and frowned when he was ignored the first time. But one firm-voice command did it, before he glanced briefly at Keelin's face and walked away.

Dermot watched him leave, and Keelin watched him watching. Then his face turned her way and he smiled softly. 'You can lean on my shoulder.'

Keelin smiled back. 'Thank you.'

He helped her upstairs with the minimum of fuss, not talking until they were halfway there and Keelin had actually allowed herself to believe that she might avoid any awkward questioning.

'You have quite an effect on Garrett, I think. Not that I can blame him.'

Keelin inwardly groaned. But managed to keep her face calm. 'I guess there aren't too many women who try to break their necks within a few days of meeting him.'

Dermot chuckled. 'No, that there isn't. But he's not alone in being affected by whatever it is, is he?'

If the ground had opened up in front of her Keelin would gladly have jumped in the hole. The last thing she wanted was a deep and meaningful conversation with Dermot on the subject of Garrett. Not when she was already having enough difficulty herself battling her emotions.

So she remained silent in the hope that he would drop it as they got closer to the hallway of bedroom doors.

'He went through a lot with Terri's mother.'

Keelin looked up at the older man. 'Yes, I know.'

'And it would be sad if the mistakes your mother and me made were repeated with you and Garrett.'

She swallowed hard and focused her gaze forwards again, her voice low. 'Yes, it would.'

They stopped in front of one of the heavy wooden doors, which Dermot pushed open to reveal a huge cast-iron bed with deep cushions and a thick duvet. He stepped back, allowing Keelin to get her balance before he released her. And then, to her astonishment, he leaned down and pressed a kiss against her cheek. 'Goodnight, child. I'm very glad you decided to make the trip to the island.'

Keelin smiled through shimmering eyes, her heart aching at the loss of a father that wasn't hers to begin with. 'Me, too.'

And as she closed the door behind her she was overwhelmed with a wave of emotion. How much simpler things would have been if Dermot had been her father and Garrett her half-brother. Then she wouldn't have had to deal with the whirlwind of conflicting emotions she felt for Garrett and the sense of somehow having disappointed Dermot by allowing him to think that she might have, in some way, led Garrett on, in order to hurt him as he had been hurt before. To cause the same kind of pain that Dermot and her mother had felt.

Thing was, she didn't really believe that she had that much of a hold on Garrett's emotions. He hadn't even tried to kiss her, not once, despite the opportunities that had been there. And although both of those things were ultimately the safer options, she still felt her heart aching that things weren't different. That the timing hadn't maybe been a little better.

Because loving a man like Garrett, and having the chance to be a part of the beautiful family he had, would have been as great a gift as she could ever have asked for.

* * *

Garrett couldn't sleep.

He tried. He even attempted counting backwards from twenty thousand, but it was to no avail. And he knew it was because, no matter how he tried to block it from his mind, he couldn't forget that Keelin was just down the hall.

How had he got so entangled with someone like her so damn quickly? That was what he'd like to know. Of all the women he had met over the past decade, why had none of them had the effect on him that she had after only a few days? It just didn't follow any logical reasoning.

And Garrett liked logic. He liked things that made sense. He didn't like being knocked off kilter. He didn't like that he was drawn to her when it would be so very much safer not to be. And most of all he hated that he was missing her before she'd even left.

A feeling that strong didn't just happen after a few days, did it? How could it? It went against everything he'd ever believed was necessary for a strong foundation for lasting love!

The minute the word 'love' entered his thoughts he angrily swung back his covers and hauled on some sweatpants. If he wasn't going to sleep then he could do some paperwork; at least *that* would be a constructive use of his mind!

In the doorway of the kitchen, he froze.

And Keelin gasped when she turned round and saw him. 'You scared me to death! I didn't hear you coming down.'

Garrett clenched his teeth and stared at her in the dimly lit room, his breath caught in his chest at the sight of her in one of *his* damned shirts!

'Where did you get that shirt?'

She glanced down at it, one hand tugging at the end as if the action might somehow make it longer than it already was. Not that it didn't cover her modestly enough, barring the expanse of naked leg. 'Terri left it out for me.'

Had she indeed? Because one of her own numerous nightdresses wouldn't have fitted Keelin's slight frame?

'How did you get down here on your own?'

She smiled. 'I'm not as much of an invalid as the Kincaid men would like to think I am. I just took a little more time than I normally would have.'

Garrett swallowed hard, his eyes glancing towards the kettle he had been on his way to boil. There was an entire room between Keelin and him, and yet he'd never felt so cornered before. If he'd been a believer in the mythical nonsense known as fate he might have thought it was out to get him.

'Do you need help getting back upstairs?'

'No.'

His gaze flickered to her face and then away again, while he pushed his hands deep into the pockets of his sweatpants. 'Can I get you anything?'

'No.' Her husky voice sounded nervous. 'I just, erm, I just wanted a glass of water. I couldn't sleep.'

And it was that nervous, almost tremulous edge to her voice that brought his gaze back to hers again.

Keelin wasn't cold, but she was shaking from shoulder to toe. She blinked back at him for several long-drawn-out seconds. *Dear, Lord.* He really was the most truly beautiful man she had ever set eyes on. And she couldn't help it. It was as if the part of her brain in charge of things like good manners and hiding the truth had temporarily shut down as her gaze tore from the intense heat in his eyes and swept lower, lingering on his mouth for a split second before they were drawn lower. Past the column of his neck, where she watched him swallowing hard, to the broad expanse of naked chest that she couldn't seem to stop looking at; rising and falling, rising and falling. The rhythm sped up the more she looked at it until she realized her breathing was matching that rhythm.

And she looked back into his eyes where the same inner battle she was waging was mirrored for her to see.

She thought he would turn and walk away. Or simply smile

and let it pass. After all, he had never taken advantage of any of the previous opportunities. But then, it had maybe never been as obvious to either of them that they were both feeling the exact same thing at the exact same time.

As her heart beat so erratically she might, given the time, have felt as if she were having a heart attack he groaned, and was across the room.

And she was in his arms.

The kiss was feverish, as if they had both been holding back for a lot longer than the time they had known each other. It was pent-up passion, and frustration, and need. And Keelin met him halfway, gave as much as she was being given, the low moan in her chest almost a sigh of completion.

This was exactly how she had known they would be. This was the kiss that she had known would sweep her off her feet and leave her branded for ever. And she had never before wanted so badly for someone to make such a strong claim on her. To say without words that she was theirs; whether it was just for that moment or for ever. To tell her as clearly as her heart could be told that never again would there be another moment like this one, another man like this one.

Garrett was taking those few minutes of her life from her. They would never be replaced, or relived. And Keelin knew that, if she lived to be a hundred and never saw him again after tonight, she would never ask for that time back again.

Just when she thought she would die from the lack of oxygen she couldn't seem to draw in fast enough, he tore his mouth from hers, and rested his forehead against hers as the sound of their joint ragged breathing filled the silent room.

Even his deep, multifaceted tone of voice was breathless. 'This is a bad idea. For both of us.'

'I know.' The words were almost wrenched from her, on a nervous exhalation of half-laughter.

His thick lashes flickered upwards as his toffee eyes searched hers up close. 'And it won't change the fact that we have different lives in different places.'

'I know that, too.'

'Or the fact that you'll leave soon.'

He hadn't voiced it as a question, hadn't said that her staying longer was an option he would like her to take. And Keelin knew that that had to be because he knew it was the truth. How could she just drop her responsibilities, her work, her legacy, and leave it all behind on the strength of a few days and a kiss like that? Even if it had been the kiss of a lifetime.

Relationships weren't founded on one kiss. Not relationships that lasted. And despite the saying that it was better to have loved and lost...

Keelin just didn't know that she could survive that kind of a loss.

'I know.'

Garrett nodded his head slightly against hers. 'This isn't something I want to be here, Keelin.'

The confession tore off a little piece of her heart. And she swallowed back the sense of rejection she felt. He didn't want to want her, that was what he was saying. What he felt was a physical attraction, not based on anything deeper. And how could it possibly be?

Just because she had been falling a little deeper every day since he had walked through the mist...

Her answer was barely a whisper. 'I know.'

His arms moved from her waist, where she had been held close, only the thin layer of shirt holding skin from skin. They lifted, and his large hands framed her face, fingers sliding into her loose hair, cradling the back of her head as his thumbs brushed against the corners of her mouth.

He tilted his head, leaning closer to angle his mouth over her parted lips, his nose nudging hers. 'But it *is* here. This is just all I'm ready to allow to happen with it...'

She sighed as his mouth brushed hers, gently this time, as if making up for the previous onslaught of passion with tenderness. But as he lifted his head a little, angled it the other way, and brushed her lips again, Keelin felt that he was taking more from her soul with that tenderness than he had with passion.

And yet she couldn't stop herself from answering touch with touch. She couldn't stop the basic instinct that brought her hands to his skin, her fingertips skimming against heat and muscle as she circled around to his back and flattened her palms to hold him to her.

Kissing Garrett was ecstasy and agony at the same time. Ecstasy of the body, agony of the heart. And she couldn't let that agony get any worse than it already was, so even though it cost her every scrap of self-control she had she pulled back from him, her head low as she lifted her hands from his skin.

'We have to stop this.'

She held her breath until he eventually answered with a gruff-voiced. 'Yes, we do.'

His fingers untangled from her hair, as with a last brush of his thumbs against her mouth he set her free and stepped back. Less than a foot away from her, he stood completely still, until Keelin had the courage to raise her chin and look at him with the best smile she could conjure up from deep, deep inside. It was the best piece of acting she had ever done.

'Don't worry.' She swallowed and damped her swollen lips as she told the biggest lie of her life. 'It was only a kiss or two. We'll both survive.'

Garrett frowned a little, for a very brief moment, nodding in agreement as he turned away. 'Exactly.'

Keelin kept her features under control, using every second of training she'd ever had on how to behave in public as she watched him walk out of the kitchen, his bare feet silent on the slate floor.

And she didn't allow the first tears to fall until she heard another door click shut and she knew it was safe to hobble back upstairs, where she allowed herself to weep silently into a pillow, for just the one night.

And she swore to herself it would be the only night she did it. Because it was immature, and completely unfounded, not to mention unrealistic—to believe that she had just had her heart irreparably broken.

CHAPTER TWELVE

GARRETT disappeared early the next morning, before Keelin came downstairs for breakfast. And although half of her was relieved, the other half felt the unspoken rejection deeply.

But then what had she expected—that he would smile and act as if nothing had happened? Could *she* have? Thing was, even if she had managed it, she would still have known it had happened. Just as he would. And pretending that nothing had happened was worse, wasn't it? Keelin knew it would hurt if it meant so little to him.

But then he had been struggling to fight his attraction to her, hadn't he? Had said himself he didn't want it there…

Keelin's head was aching from the constant thinking.

And from the fact that Dermot was hell-bent she wasn't leaving until she could walk without a limp. After more than an hour of debate he met her halfway with a compromise of one more night, and some of her belongings from the hotel. Including her pyjamas. If she was going to get caught again by Garrett in the middle of the night, then she was going to make sure she was covered from head to toe! And not in an article of clothing belonging to *him*.

When Dermot and Terri came in for lunch after clearing up some farm chores, they found Keelin at the table with her mother's letters, sandwiches and a fresh chocolate cake laid out in preparation for their return.

'You baked a cake?' Terri reached out to cut a slice and promptly found her hand swatted away by Keelin.

'Yes, I did. For *after* the sandwiches. Go wash those hands.'

'You didn't have to do that, you know.' Dermot smiled at her from the sink as he washed *his* hands. 'Not that I'm going to say I'm sorry you did.'

'Well, I have to do something to earn my keep.'

Terri grinned at her. 'No, seriously, *you* baked a cake?'

Keelin laughed up at him. 'Why is that such a surprise exactly? Don't I look like the kind of woman who can bake a cake if she wants to?'

'No.'

She laughed again, leaning forwards to stage whisper. 'I'm not. It's my friend Ally's idiot's recipe. You don't even have to have a measuring jug…'

Terri, with a grin still on her face, leaned closer until their heads were almost touching, her voice a matching whisper. 'I might need that.'

'Remind me and I'll write it down before I leave.'

There was a flicker of something across Terri's face as she leaned back. But before Keelin could decipher it she had gone to wash her hands as ordered and Keelin was distracted as Dermot pulled out a chair, his head nodding in the direction of the letters.

'Still reading them, then?'

'Yes.' She stroked them with the palm of her hand. 'Can't seem to put them down now I've started. You wrote to each other for a long time.'

Another nod. 'The last one was not long after you were born. They kind of petered off after that. Our lives went in different directions.'

'Did you love her, Gramps?' Terri plunked down onto the chair next to Keelin, her hand reaching out for sandwiches. 'Keelin's mum. I mean, really, really love her?'

Keelin was embarrassed on Dermot's behalf.

But Dermot seemed unfazed. 'Aye, that I did.'

'Did she love you?'

Dermot's eyes met Keelin's across the table and Keelin answered. 'Yes, she did.'

'Then how come she left?'

It was an echo of the question Garrett had asked her the day before as he'd carried her back to the house. And as tempted as she had been to flick through the letters to find the answer, Keelin knew that a big part of it could be threaded through them, so she was taking her time and reading every word.

'I don't know yet; I haven't got to the end.'

Dermot shrugged. 'I could just tell you.'

'No, don't you dare! I already know she left. But it's a little like seeing a movie and then reading the book. You know what the outcome is, but you want to read all the bits the movie missed so you get a fuller story.'

Terri looked intrigued, her mouth full of sandwich as she spoke. 'Can I read them after you?'

'No you can't. They're Keelin's mother's. They're *private*.' Dermot smiled indulgently at his granddaughter. 'You know, private as in that piece of paper you have pinned to your bedroom door?'

Terri shrugged and chewed for a while, her eyes on the forbidden letters as she thought. 'So, was it like, you know, love at first sight? Like in the movies like Keelin said?'

Keelin laughed again. 'Oh, I don't think I said anything about love at first sight.'

'Not a believer in it, then?'

Her gaze flickered back to Dermot's face in surprise. Surely a man as sensible and with the wisdom brought by experience knew better than to believe in such a fantasy?

'No, I'm afraid I'm not. Are you going to tell me you are?'

Another shrug. 'Stranger things have happened. Some people get married after a few weeks of meeting each other.'

'And divorce a few months after that.'

'Not all of them.'

'Ninety-nine point nine per cent of them. There's no way you can know someone well enough after a few weeks to know whether or not you can stay with them for the rest of your life.'

Terri seemed fascinated by the topic. 'How long *do* you have to know them? I should know these things, don't you think?'

Keelin smiled indulgently at her. 'Longer than five minutes, sweetheart, trust me.'

'I knew after five minutes how I felt about your mother.'

'You couldn't possibly have!' Keelin was astonished, her heart skipping a little beat in surprise. 'You couldn't have known what kind of person she was, or what she wanted from life, or whether or not you were suited. All those things matter.'

He nodded very slowly, his gaze steady as he smiled at her obvious shock. 'Yes, I'm not saying they don't. And after a few hours of talking to her I knew that those things were there, too. But love doesn't always follow reasoning; sometimes it's just there. And it's up to the person to decide whether or not they trust it enough to try it. Just as many people fall for people they wouldn't ordinarily look twice at, don't have anything in common with and yet they're a perfect match. Live happily ever after despite the odds…'

Terri nodded firmly. 'I believe in love at first sight. I think it's romantic.'

'It's not romantic if it leads to heartache.'

Dermot's smile changed a little, the look in his eyes one of

melancholy. 'Well, it doesn't always have a happy ending, I'll
grant you that.'

Keelin's breath caught. 'I'm sorry, Dermot. I didn't mean—'

'I know you didn't.' He reached out for the knife to cut some
cake, glancing up at her very briefly. 'You read the letters,
child. And then we'll talk some more about it. Might just make
sense of a lot of things for you—you never know.'

While Keelin's aching brain struggled with what exactly he
meant by that, her lips parting in anticipation of some words
Terri leaned forwards, her face animated. 'We're gonna go meet
Dad up at the new house. You have to come see it; it's gorgeous!'

The mention of the absent Garrett was enough to make
Keelin catch her breath. Just the smallest mention of him was
all it took now? Terrific.

'I thought you lived here?'

Terri shook her head. 'Nah, not 'til last year. We're rebuild-
ing our own house. Dad says we don't want to cramp Gramps
style for too long. He has to have his own place so he can go
out and find me a nice Grandma. The kind that spoils grand-
daughters silly.'

Keelin smiled affectionately. 'I'd quite like one of those.'

'The grandma or the granddaughter?'

'Oh, one of each would be nice.'

'Stay here, then. Don't leave, and you can share my new
grandma with me and maybe after a few years you can get the
other one.' Terri winked as she grabbed some cake. 'Come on,
come see the house, *please?*'

She didn't just go because Terri pleaded so hard. For so long
She did it because she genuinely *did* want to see the house that
Garrett was building, so that she could picture it in her mind if
she wanted to after she left. And the first time she saw him again
she wanted it to be somewhere that *wasn't* the kitchen...

What she wasn't prepared for as her eyes followed the running Terri's progress all the way into her father's arms was the sight of him in his office clothes.

Wow. He should wear a shirt and jacket all the time as far as Keelin was concerned. But then there was how good he looked in his long waxed coat, or the shirt the same color as his eyes, or, minus any shirt at all…

She had to swallow hard. This really had to stop. She couldn't go drooling over him more and more every time she saw him. It was pathetic. She couldn't go holding her breath until he stopped swinging his daughter in circles, his deep laughter floating across the air, while she waited for him to look across and see her. And she so very definitely couldn't have her heart beating so hard in anticipation of a smile, no matter how small, that might say they could get past what had happened the night before.

But for every moment that she was attracted by the way he looked there were the ten moments when she just wanted to listen to his voice, to have him share details of his life with her, or just tease her with his sparkling warm eyes and his inimitable way of knocking her off kilter.

Such a conglomeration of moments that her brain said she had no business feeling so fast and so strong. It just made absolutely no sense.

But love doesn't always follow reasoning, sometimes it's just there.

Dermot's words echoed in her mind as Garrett stopped swinging Terri, took a moment to listen to what she was saying. Then his chin lifted, and he looked directly at Keelin.

And smiled a small half-smile that said it was all right for her to come to him.

Keelin smiled back; she couldn't not. Yep. Sometimes it *was* just there. Even if it did inevitably lead to heartache in the long term.

* * *

Garrett was still lit up inside with the sheer joy of having Terri run into his arms to be swung as she had when she was little. It had been such a long time since she'd done it, since she had temporarily shrugged the mantle of pseudo-adult in favour of a moment of childlike affection. And, for him, it was a rare and precious moment.

One he knew had probably been made possible by Keelin, and her attempts at bridge-building.

So that when he looked up and saw her he forgot himself for a moment, and allowed his happiness to show in half a smile.

Happiness that maybe wasn't solely related to the gift he'd just received from Terri, but probably equally related to seeing Keelin.

Even if just looking at her brought a swift reminder of how much it had cost him to walk away from her the night before. And he hated himself for that weakness.

But apparently it didn't stop him from being glad to see her again, or from feeling the sudden sense of pride at being able to show her his new home.

So he could do what, this time? Try and impress her again? This time with his ability to provide a home should she by some miracle, overnight, become the kind of woman who could be content in a place like Valentia? Just because of the fact that last night he'd surrendered his self-control long enough to do what he had wanted to do since he had first set eyes on her?

And yet here he was *again*, walking swiftly to her side before she tried to limp over the makeshift bridge they'd made over the stream. So that he could help her *again* when she most likely didn't want his help, so that he could reach out for her as he did, *again*, his palm held upwards in silent invitation between them.

Her large blue eyes stared at it for a long time before she hesitantly fit her hand into his, her fingers curling around his, trusting her slight weight to his care as she made her way across to him.

'How's the ankle feeling?' He allowed her to free her hand from his, immediately curling his fingers into his palm as if, subconsciously, he thought he might somehow trap some of the warmth of her touch there.

She tilted her chin up and shot him a somewhat shy gaze. 'A little better, I think. Not quite ready for the Olympics just yet.'

'No, wouldn't have thought so.' He stood back a little and held an arm out to his side in invitation before adjusting his longer stride to her even shorter than usual one while he fought to find something to say.

But she seemed content to stay silent, so he took that to mean he could, too. It was certainly the easier option.

As they came past the line of trees and the house came into view he held back a little, looking at her face from the corner of his eye. *Waiting.*

He smiled broadly when her eyes widened.

'It's *beautiful.*'

'Yes, I quite like it, too.' He looked up at the large house, the old stone façade blending it into the scenery as if it had always been there, rather than the few months that it had. 'I figured if I wanted Terri to see a future here then I needed to give her a place of her own for that future. It's been a long time since I've relied so heavily on Dermot to help take care of her.'

Keelin dragged her gaze away from the house and he felt her eyes on him as she spoke. 'He'll miss you though. Both of you.'

'We won't be all that far away. It was just time, that's all. And we'll see him every day. I think he'll be quite glad of the peace and quiet in the evenings.'

She suddenly stopped walking, so that Garrett was forced to do the same, having got a couple of feet ahead of her. He turned, stepped back towards her, his brows lifting in question. 'Do you need to rest a minute?'

She shook her head. 'No, I keep telling you I'm not an invalid. It's not that; it's…'

It wasn't like her not to speak her mind, he knew that much at the very least. And Garrett was suddenly uneasy. 'It's what? Come on, I'd like to hear what you think.'

Her long lashes fluttered upwards as she searched his face. 'You can't keep choosing her future for her. How can someone as intelligent as you are not understand that?'

That was what he got for wanting to know. He frowned at her reasoning. 'I'm not.'

'Aren't you?' She waved a hand towards the house. 'You've just built a house for her. That's what you said. You've made it more difficult for her to choose her own path, if her choice is to be away from here. It's emotional blackmail, Garrett. Don't you see?'

'No.' He shook his head. 'I don't. You think by making a home for her that I'm saying she should stay with me for the rest of her life? Yes, this will be hers when I'm not here any more. And, yes, this is my way of making sure she always has the security of knowing she has a place that is hers. Regardless of what happens in her life. But it's not some premeditated plan to lock her away in a modern-day tower.'

Her gaze flickered to the house as she thought some more, and then back to his face as she asked. 'And what are *you* then—a caretaker? You're just going to rattle round in this house on your own 'til you're old and grey, waiting for her to come back and claim it?'

Was that what he'd thought he would do? He really didn't think it was. It would mean admitting, at thirty-four, that he had somehow already dismissed the idea of ever making any kind of a life for himself beyond what he already had. And he didn't believe that, did he? No, he didn't. He'd always believed he would meet someone like—

His frown grew.

But had he been building a place that subconsciously he had hoped to share with someone else? Someone he could *grow* old and grey with, who could maybe help him to add to the family he already had? Someone like—

Garrett dearly wanted to hit something.

He looked over his shoulder at the house, frowning hard at the two options his mind had come up with. And the fact that they had both come back to the same thing.

Keelin's voice sounded a little closer, lower, more intimate, touching at a chord inside him that ached like a very old wound.

'Are you going to punish yourself your whole life for something that wasn't your fault?'

'You *really* don't know what you're talking about.'

Her voice remained soft, despite the harsh warning tone in his.

'Then tell me I'm wrong. Tell me that building something this far ahead of time for Terri isn't your way of trying to plan her life in a place you see as safe for her. You can't protect her from everything in life; she has to get to make her own mistakes. And loving her means letting her see that you're as capable of taking a chance on being happy as she should, doesn't it? It doesn't mean shutting yourself off and never reaching out for what you really want. Don't do that to yourself.'

He swung round to face her, resentment building in the pit of his stomach. 'You think you can just waltz in here, psychoanalyze my life in a few days and then leave everything all neatly tied up in a ribbon before you go?' He shook his head. 'The life you have planned for yourself once you leave here must be just perfect. I'm surprised you've managed to stay here for as long as you have if it keeps you from that road to bliss!'

Keelin's eyes widened. 'You have no idea what my life will be when I leave here any more than I ultimately do.'

'Well, tell me where you get off informing me what it is I'm doing with mine without even asking what *I* want?'

'You haven't *denied* it!' Her voice rose. '*Don't* you want a life of your own, Garrett? Don't you want to meet someone and just take a *chance* on being happy with them? On having more kids as amazing as the one you've already got? How can you *not* want that?'

He stepped closer, towering over her as he leaned his face closer. 'You think that it would be any of your business if I *did?* Or who I might want that *with?* After all, what was the phrase you used: 'Only a kiss or two'? That's as far as you and me go.'

She visibly baulked.

So he tilted his head and pushed even harder. 'You tell *me*, Keelin, why should it matter a damn to you what happens to me when you're not here any more? This is just a stop-off point for you on the road to some great plan you have for a better life than Valentia could ever possibly offer in your mind. If I choose to spend my life here alone or if I choose to marry and have a dozen more kids, it doesn't really matter to you, does it?'

And his heart thundered agonizingly in his chest as he waited for her answer, while he felt wave after wave of anger and resentment rolling over him. Resentment at her so astutely pointing out to his mind the one thing he had been avoiding facing up to himself.

That she then felt the need to try and fix those things before she left with some magical wave of her hand...well... that just made him feel—*foolish*. Foolish for wanting what he so plainly couldn't have.

Who else but a masochistic fool would care so deeply so fast for someone who had never, ever been about to stay and take a chance on him?

And being made to feel like that kind of a fool just made him resent her all the more...

She continued to look up at him with wide eyes, the tiniest flicker of her lashes the only give-away that she was feeling anything. And it hit Garrett that he couldn't see so clearly into the windows to her soul as he had for a while, as if she had closed some kind of shutter and blocked him out. To hide something, maybe? But what?

'Keelin! Keelin, come see my room!'

Her gaze shifted to Terri at the front door of the house as she raised a hand to wave at her. 'I'll be right there.'

With a brief upwards look she took a step past him. But he stopped her, his hand capturing her elbow and tugging her closer. 'You haven't answered my question.'

She wrenched her elbow free, glaring up at him venomously. 'Which question *was* that exactly?'

'Why it should matter a damn to you what I do or don't do and who with when you won't be here.'

And he found a tiny, well-buried part of himself almost waiting, hoping that she might give him the answer he wanted the most.

'No, you're right.' She continued glaring up into his eyes, the gaze almost boring a hole in him as she answered his question with tight lips. 'It's none of my business what you do or who with when I'm not here. But it doesn't stop me from caring, Garrett. I just, for the life of me right now this minute, don't have the faintest idea why I *should* care.'

CHAPTER THIRTEEN

IT TOOK over half an hour of touring the house with Terri, Garrett silent and sullen behind them, before Keelin stopped hurting from his stinging words and found an ache of a different kind to focus on.

If she had thought the house was beautiful on the outside, then the inside was a whole new level above that.

Every window at the back of the house faced the ocean so that it was flooded with light, every piece of wood on the floor shone with a deep patina that exuded warmth, every piece of furniture, every lamp and every picture on the wall created an atmosphere of elegant simplicity that struck a chord inside Keelin. A yearning that said *home* to her.

Garrett had built a home.

A home that he would either stay in alone until Terri decided where her place in the world truly was, or that he would fill with more small versions of himself with deep chocolate tousled hair and warm toffee eyes, who would fill the rooms with their laughter, the echoes of their feet on the wooden floors, their voices ringing from room to room as the house echoed with love.

And every fibre of Keelin's being wanted the latter for him. Even while walking through each room was like some kind of an ideal home exhibition selling happily ever after, in her own mind. One that just wasn't meant to be and never would be, *for her.*

She caught sight of the painting as she turned from the ocean view and avoided looking directly at Garrett's face by focusing on a point over his shoulder. And her feet carried her forwards as if she were drawn to it by some invisible sense of inevitability.

'Keelin?' Terri walked up to her side, tilting her head to study Keelin's face. 'What's wrong? You look sad.'

Keelin turned her gaze from the painting to smile tremulously at Terri, her throat thick so that her first attempt at speaking failed and she had to clear her throat to try again. 'Do you know where this painting came from?'

'Dad?' Terri ducked her chin round Keelin so she could look at her father. 'Wasn't this Gramps' painting from the other house? You know, it used to be in the hall upstairs?'

The air displaced at Keelin's other shoulder as Garrett stepped closer, his deep voice sending a shiver of awareness along her spine. 'Yes. It was a wedding present when he married Mum. I remember that, because there was a whole fuss when it arrived special delivery. Mum was thrilled. She'd never had a piece of original art before.'

Keelin looked at it again, studying each brush stroke, the use of colour, her eyes searching for a signature that wasn't there. But she didn't need a signature to know.

Garrett's voice lowered again, softer this time, as if some of the anger of their argument was finally dissipating. 'It's a view from the island. Not far past the lighthouse, I think. Dermot said it should have a better place to show it off. He even picked what wall it went on.'

It took a moment more before he took a deep breath, exhaling the words. 'And it's your mother's, isn't it?'

Keelin nodded, then flashed a very brief smile up at his

face. 'I hope you have it well insured. It's unsigned but there's no doubting it's her work.'

'You know all of her work that well?'

'I should do. I'm an art appraiser, it's my job to know her work inside out, and hundreds of others, too.'

'I didn't know that.'

'No, you wouldn't, you never asked.' She bestowed him another small smile, this time a more rueful one. 'Though I did maybe give the impression that full-time spoilt little rich girl was my profession.'

'You never said spoilt. And I think we both know you weren't. You earned your keep.'

'Wouldn't have been too much of a life long term, though, would it? And it made sense to study art when I lived with an artist. It gave us plenty to talk about and debate once I got through my rebellious stage.'

Garrett took a long moment to think over the new information, before nodding and asking. 'So is that what you're going back to?'

In an instinctive impulse to fight hurt with hurt, she smirked briefly up at him, her voice dropping. 'Doesn't really matter, does it?'

It was as much as she would say in front of Terri. But it was enough; he'd got what she meant. And the answering flash of anger in his eyes was swift.

Which should have made the devil on her shoulder hoot with glee, but it didn't. It just made her throat thicken again as she fought back her earlier hurt. So she focused on the painting again,

'This is an early piece, just at the end of her landscape period, I'd guess.' She tilted her head as she looked it over. 'But it's a one-off. I'll even bet she did it especially for Dermot when she heard he was getting married. And as a one-off, rare, even *unsigned* piece, it's worth a fortune at auction now that she's gone.'

'How much?' Terri grinned up at her. 'Like major-shopping-trip fortune or round-the-world-trip fortune? 'Cos I'll take either, you know…'

Keelin smiled. 'Sweetheart, it's a round-trip-and-the-value-of-this-house fortune for a painting this size. And that's before you even inherit it, years from now when it might even be worth enough for you to take an early retirement from whatever you'd decided to do.'

'It's not for sale.'

She turned to look into Garrett's eyes again. 'Oh, I think you might want to reconsider *that* decision.'

He stared at her with the toffee eyes she now knew so well, the angry silence he'd been wearing on his features replaced with an intense sincerity.

'It was a housewarming gift to us from Dermot. I don't care about its monetary value.'

'I can understand that, but I don't know that you'll want it *here*.' She tore her gaze from his eyes back to the painting, stepping closer to look at the right-hand corner before she lifted a finger and pointed. 'Because, you see that little girl playing with the ribbon? That's me. My mother put me on Valentia before I even knew where it was.'

Terri gasped behind her, stepping closer to wrap an arm around Keelin's waist, that without thinking Keelin then matched with the same simple embrace.

'Do you think she knew you'd come here one day?'

She could feel her eyes filling with yet another set of tears. Was she going to do nothing on this island but cry? For the mother she had lost, for the father that had never been hers, for the man she couldn't hold onto even if he had wanted to try to hold onto her?

It just wasn't fair. How could her mother have painted this picture? This *lie?*

And then, with a flash of insight, she suddenly *knew.* 'I think she painted this for Dermot, maybe even before she heard he was getting married. It can take weeks and weeks to do one this size. And I think it was her goodbye. Her way of saying sorry. By showing him a little glimpse of what might have been. In some other world, given the same set of choices, she might have stayed. And I could have been born here. That would have been me playing on the island I lived on, because I'd have grown up here with my mother and Dermot together.'

Where she might have met Garrett earlier. Where they might have had a chance to spend time getting to know each other without the barriers they now had between them. And, who knew? They might have really fallen in love, believed in it, trusted it to be real. And then Terri might have been Keelin's daughter too…

But it was a pipedream, a fantasy, a make-believe world of happily ever after to go with the happily-ever-after house that Garrett had built. To maybe, one day soon, live in with someone else. Someone he could love with all of that intensity he possessed and who could love him in return. And spend *years* getting to know him.

Keelin forced another smile for Terri before she stepped away, turning and walking past Garrett without even looking at him. Because she was afraid he might see. He might look into her eyes, and, as raw and vulnerable as she was in that moment, he might see how much she wanted to *be* that woman.

She was halfway across the room before he spoke.

'Keelin—'

Her cell phone rang.

It took a moment for her to recognize the sound, because it seemed like for ever since she had last heard it. She'd even forgotten she had it in her coat pocket.

Retrieving it, she glanced briefly at the screen, then equally briefly at Garrett's frowning face, before she flipped it open with a flick of her wrist. 'Jackson, hi.'

When she didn't move out of the room, Garrett looked back at the painting, as if studying it for the millionth time would make him recognize Keelin better. Had some part of his subconscious mind been looking at that painting for years, while it had hung in the house he had grown up in, so that when he'd seen her that first day on the lane he had already known who she was?

Was that why he'd felt that immediate fascination with her? That sense of mystery that he couldn't quite figure out that had drawn him to her?

Had he just been trying to 'place her' in his memory?

Keelin's tone of voice changed slightly after she sighed. 'Yes, I know. The reception here is very bad. This is the first time it has rung in days. No, I didn't get any messages. I just told you—bad reception.'

It would be a more rational explanation for Garrett's mind. Much more rational than knowing someone for less than a week and feeling the way he did. Because it couldn't be love he felt. *Couldn't possibly be.*

Maybe if she stayed a little longer he could know one way or the other? But that would mean asking her to stay, wouldn't it?

'They can't make that decision without me, Jackson.'

Garrett watched as she frowned. And he wondered if she would frown like that if he invited her to stay longer. He had asked someone to stay only the one time before. And that had led to arguments, pain, things said in the heat of the moment that could never be taken back...

'When? What time tomorrow? Jackson—yes, but a little more warning would have— Fine. Right. I'll be there.' Her eyes rose and locked with Garrett's.

And Garrett felt his heart twist so painfully it almost took the air from his lungs. How did she *do* that?

How did she floor him every time with a single glance?

But even as he finally admitted to himself that the irrational answer was the only true answer to that question, she sighed, and said the words he'd been waiting for her to say all along.

'I'll leave this evening.'

'You can't leave yet!' Terri reacted before Garrett could.

And he closed his eyes for a second. This was exactly what he had hoped wouldn't happen. 'Terri—'

'But our shopping day?'

The colour had drained from Keelin's face, and Garrett knew as he dragged his gaze from her to the anguished face of his daughter that she knew what she had just done. 'Keelin can't help it if she's needed back.'

'But—' Terri's mouth thinned as she pursed her lips together, glancing up at the roof as she fought to keep her disappointment back. But it was too late, they all knew how much she had wanted that one day. 'Fine. Have a good trip.'

'Terri—' Keelin stepped forwards as Terri fled the room, her attempt at following halted by Garrett's stern tone.

'Leave her be. She'll be all right in a while.'

Keelin's voice trembled. 'But she was so looking forward to it. And I promised her.'

'Well, it's maybe just as well she didn't get any more attached to you than she already is. Your leaving was always going to hurt.' And he knew, even as he said it, that it wasn't just Terri he was referring to.

And as if she somehow sensed that, Keelin's wide eyes rose and studied his for a long moment. 'I don't have a choice, Garrett. I have to go. I'm the trustee of my mother's estate, and that includes all of her works. I can't not—'

'Continue to live your life through her in the same way you just accused me of doing with Terri?' He could hear the bitterness in his tone, couldn't stop it from being there.

She inhaled sharply. 'That legacy was entrusted to me. Who else will safeguard it for the future if I don't?'

'So you'll what? Stand guard over it for the rest of your life?'

She stepped closer, her eyes blazing with anger, and something more. The shutter dropped again so that he could see the play of emotions to their fullest. 'And why would it matter to you what I do with the rest of my life when I'm not here any more? In just the same way as it shouldn't matter to me if you—'

'Waste my life looking after this place as a caretaker?' His burst of laughter held a hint of sarcasm. 'But isn't that exactly what you are? What you've been your entire life. You're the caretaker of your mother's life. You live vicariously through her. So I don't really think that qualifies you to throw stones at my choices, do you?'

'Well, you see, that's where you're wrong, Garrett. It's *exactly* what qualifies me. Because I know what it's like to be so tied to a parent and their hopes, expectations and legacies that you never take a chance on something you might want for yourself! There's *no one* better qualified than me. Because if I *had* the choice, right this minute, I'd—'

'You'd *what,* Keelin?' This time he stepped closer, so that he was once again towering over her, once again close enough to be surrounded by her sweet scent, to be so close that his body almost touched her.

And Keelin stared at him with wide eyes, her breathing fast and shallow as once again the conflicting emotions flickered across her eyes. She lifted her chin, ran the pink end of her tongue over her lips so that Garrett focused his gaze there while he waited for her to answer.

The shutters in her eyes came back while he fought the urge to kiss her again. One last time. So that the last memory she would have of her visit would be of him and of passion and mutual wanting. Because they might not have a foundation for anything else but they had that, didn't they?

But the shutters were there when he looked back into her eyes; the moment was lost. And maybe it was better that it was.

So Garrett shook his head at his own foolishness and stepped back, his voice flat and calm so that she wouldn't know how, for the briefest flickering second, he had thought she might say, given the choice, she would have stayed.

'Dermot is talking to the landscaper outside. He'll take you back to the hotel.' He tried not to look at her, he really did. But he couldn't help it. Just one last time.

The eyes that had once been so expressive were dead, as if she wasn't even seeing him any more.

So he took a breath and turned away. 'Look out for that ankle when you're driving.'

'It's an automatic.'

'You'll be fine, then.'

'No, actually—' she turned away and mumbled the words as she walked past him '—I doubt I'll ever be fine again.'

CHAPTER FOURTEEN

'WHAT are you doing here? Are you on your own? Oh, please tell me you didn't get here on your own?'

There was only a brief nod in reply as Keelin climbed the last stone step to get to her.

So Keelin softened her voice. 'What happened?' Before she swallowed back the bubble of panic in her throat. 'Does your dad know you're here?'

Terri shook her head again. 'We had our first big grown-up fight yesterday.'

'And you ran away?'

'I wanted to see you.'

She smiled down at Terri's forlorn expression. 'Let's go inside. We'll phone your dad first, so he knows you're safe, and then we'll talk.'

And that phone call couldn't be made fast enough for Garrett, Keelin knew that. How frantic must he be? Or more to the point how much worse would he be when he knew where she was? For her to have made the trip across the country alone certainly showed tenacity, ingenuity and determination, but it had also been foolish, reckless and possibly even a little selfish. The latter three no doubt being what Garrett would focus on.

Keelin knew he would probably say it was her fault. If she

had never made the trip to Valentia, if she had never met them all, if she hadn't befriended Terri…

But Keelin wasn't going to apologize for any of those things. She did, however, force Terri to make the call. If she was going to do something this serious, then she had to face the consequences of her actions.

'And tell him I'll bring you back.'

Walking down the hall so as not to eavesdrop, she sighed loudly. This was the worst thing that could have happened. Now she would have to go back to Valentia, when leaving it had cost her so much a week ago, and she'd have to see Garrett again, which would be risky at best.

Because she'd almost managed to persuade herself she couldn't possibly have felt so much for him so quickly. Even if he was a constant shadow in the background every day now, like words spoken in a whisper she was straining to hear all the time but couldn't quite make out.

And then there were her dreams, when she would awaken in the middle of the night in the empty house with only the background noise of the city while she lay alone and tried to discover what it was that had woken her.

'He wants to speak to you.' Terri handed her the phone and mouthed a 'sorry'.

Keelin's heart fluttered as she took the phone, her pulse beating erratically as she stepped away from Terri and tried to keep her voice calm.

'Hello, Garrett.'

There was a moment of silence from the other end before he answered her in a husky voice.

'Hello, Keelin.' She heard him take a breath. 'I'm sorry about this. I had no idea she'd go all the way to you.'

Keelin shot Terri a small frown before she placed a hand over the mouthpiece and instructed her on where to find the kitchen and the kettle. Then she sat down on the heavily engraved wooden bench hugging one wall of the hall, kicking her heels off her aching feet while she spoke.

'You have to have been frantic. If I'd thought she would do this I would never have left her my address. It was supposed to be so she could write if she wanted to.'

'I know. And it's not your fault.'

There was another long, uneasy silence. Then Keelin tried to control her breathing before speaking again. 'Can I ask what the argument was about?'

'She didn't tell you?'

'No, I just got here and she was on the doorstep so the first thing I did was get her to ring you.'

Another pause, then. 'Thank you.'

And the deep multifaceted baritone of his voice, accompanied with that husky edge, almost killed Keelin. Lord, but she had missed that voice. She had missed *him*.

She'd been kidding herself if she thought what she felt was any less real or less strong than it had been when she'd been there with him, hadn't she?

'I can come and get her.'

'No, you're busy. And I've cleared up the work I had to do. We appointed a board of trustees today, so I don't mind making the trip. She has to have come here because she needed to talk, and we'll have the perfect opportunity to do that on the way back.'

She frowned a little as she realized that she'd automatically stepped back into the role of Terri's confidante without considering how Garrett might feel about that. So she took a breath and added, 'If that's all right with you, that is?'

'For you to talk to her? Yes, it's all right.'

'It's just that the last time I saw you we didn't exactly part as friends…'

Another long pause. 'She's missed you.'

How much would Keelin have given for that 'she' to be a 'we' or an 'I'? For the freedom that those words would have given her to tell him that she missed him, too.

'I've missed her, too. And I know that may seem silly when I hardly had the time to get to know her properly...'

'It was long enough for you to make a lasting impression.' Another deep breath. 'She needs an adult female in her life right now more than I had realized before you came along. And you have a lot in common with her.'

'Yes, yes, I suppose I do.'

There was yet another long pause, and Keelin squirmed a little on the hard bench she was sitting on. It was the most awkward telephone conversation she had ever had. And it didn't help that in each of those pauses her heart was clamouring for her to fill the gaps with all the things she wasn't saying to him.

'Well, I guess I'll see you when you get here.'

Her heart leapt in anticipation, then settled like a dead weight in her chest as it realized there would be more heartache along the way, too. Because she'd have to go through leaving all over again.

'All right. We'll be there in a few hours.'

'Okay.'

She kept the receiver to her ear for a long time, convinced she could still hear him breathing at the other end, and reluctant to be the first one to hang up, until there was a 'click' and the line went dead.

Then she sat there for several minutes, staring into nothingness as she tried to mentally prepare herself for the reunion. And the inevitable anguish that would follow her departure. This time had to be the last time; she just couldn't keep doing this to herself. She couldn't spend her life feeling as if she were dead inside because she couldn't hear his voice or look into his eyes.

Terri appeared with two cups of tea and a look of apology. 'Did he yell at you?'

'No, he didn't yell.' She took one of the cups and shook her head before patting the bench beside her, waiting until Terri was seated before she spoke again. 'You have to know how much this would have scared him, though. You're his life, Terri; he loves you so much. If anything had happened...'

The young girl's shoulders slumped as the innuendo hung in the air between them, her chin dropping to study her trainer-clad feet. 'I know he loves me. I love him, too. I just wish he would trust me and realize that I'm not some little kid any more.'

'It can't be easy for him to accept that. You've been his little girl all your life.' Keelin lifted her hand and tucked a thick lock of dark chocolate hair behind Terri's ear. 'No parent gets it right one hundred per cent of the time, no matter how hard they try. What you've got to remember is that everything he does and says is meant for the best. He's trying. You just have to allow that sometimes he'll make mistakes. Just like you will. Like you did by not telling him where you were going when you came here.'

When her chin rose her eyes were already filling with tears. 'He wouldn't have let me come.'

Keelin's heart tore. Of course he wouldn't have. Even if Keelin had left on better terms with him, there was still the fact that she lived so far away, and in the city. And in his mind there wouldn't have been enough of a foundation for Terri to have wanted so badly to see her.

But the amount of time didn't seem to matter a damn for the level of attachment that had grown between them, not in Terri's mind, and most definitely not in Keelin's. Time hadn't made *any* difference to *her* forming a forceful attachment to *either* of them...

'You still should have asked him.'

'I know.' She sniffed loudly. 'I just really wanted to talk to you and he didn't want me to.'

Keelin's eyes widened, her hand stilling the smoothing of Terri's hair. 'He told you you couldn't talk to me?'

'He said that you had a life of your own and you were probably too busy for me.'

He had said that? How could he do that? How dared he? How dared he take the argument between them and use it as a way of controlling his own child again? Did he really think that she would be so badly influenced by Keelin? Or that Keelin would ever have rejected her or hurt her in any way?

Did his level of contempt at his own weakness in having been physically attracted to her go so deep?

Keelin couldn't have been any more hurt if someone had kicked her in the chest.

When she didn't say anything straight away Terri swiped at her cheeks and smiled weakly up at her. 'He's been like a bear with a sore head since you left.'

Still reeling from such a massive rejection from Garrett, Keelin chose to ignore what that might mean in an ideal fairy-tale world, instead setting her cup down to draw Terri into her arms. 'I'll talk to your dad. But you have to promise me you'll never pull a stunt like this again. If you want to talk to me I'll only ever be a phone call away. I promise you. Any time, about anything. I'll be here for you.'

Terri's arms snaked around Keelin's waist and she held on tight, nestling her head in against her shoulder. 'Did he make you leave? Did you go because you don't like him?'

'No.' Keelin picked a point on the ceiling to focus on as she swallowed the lump in her throat. 'No, I left because I had things I had to do.'

Her head rose from Keelin's shoulder. 'You had a fight, though, didn't you?'

'Yes, we did. We don't agree on absolutely everything. I don't think two people ever do.'

'Gramps had a fight with him too, after you left. He said he was a bloody idiot for making the same mistake as he had.'

Keelin grimaced as Terri repeated what had been said. And it wasn't just from her use of the words 'bloody idiot'. It had much more to do with the fact that she had managed to cause a ripple effect through that family even after she had left. She had never meant to do so much harm.

She squeezed her arms a little tighter around Terri. 'I'm sorry that happened and that you had to hear it. I really am. I never meant to cause any arguments.'

Terri nodded. 'It was because he let you go like Gramps let your Mum go, wasn't it?'

'That was different; they loved each other.'

'Couldn't you love my dad, Keelin? If you got to know him a little better, I mean.' She smiled up at her, a look of hope in her toffee eyes. 'He's not that bad really. And he looks okay, you know, for someone his age. All my school friends think so. And we have this great new house—'

'Terri—' Keelin's voice caught. How could she tell her that she already loved Garrett, that it wasn't *her* feelings that were the problem?

Terri's eyes darkened and she nodded sadly. 'I know. I'm sorry. It's not any of my business. Dad said that, too. But it just would have been so cool to have you as my mum. I'd have loved that.'

Garrett was standing in the doorway as they got to the gate where he had first held her in his arms. And Keelin's eyes rose slowly, taking in the sight of him from his feet to the top of his head while she temporarily forgot how to breathe. She shouldn't have been surprised really, should she?

Because even though she was so very hurt by him forbidding Terri to have any contact with her, it still didn't take away from everything else.

He had thought he was conducting damage control, and, even though it had been wrong, he had done it out of love for his daughter. Even if that love could be entirely too protective at times.

But he was still just a man trying to do what he thought was best, a man who had managed to raise the kind of blossoming adult who would be a credit to him, a man who cared for so many things and took on the responsibility for their long-term welfare. Even if one of those things wasn't and never would be Keelin herself.

And he still had that intensity about him as his eyes locked with hers across the small distance between them.

Terri turned around and hugged Keelin tight, her voice a whisper in Keelin's ear. 'Thank you. For everything. For bringing me home and for the talk on the way back. I love you.'

The sentiment didn't seem the tiniest bit out of place to Keelin. And she smiled that she was free to express how she felt so openly and easily. 'I love you too, sweetheart. And we'll talk again soon, I promise.'

Drawing back a little, she framed one side of Terri's face with her hand, leaning in to add. 'Talk to your dad about all this stuff too, please? For me? He'll listen. Just be patient with him; he's trying his best.'

Terri blinked back tears as she smiled. 'I know.'

Keelin then wrapped her arms around her body to cover the emptiness she felt inside as she watched Terri walk up the path and into Garrett's waiting arms. She swallowed back the hard lump in her throat, forcing back the hot tears in the backs of her eyes while she watched Garrett's eyes close, the look of relief on his face enough to break Keelin in two.

Her heart tore when his eyes opened again, immediately seeking her out and holding her answering gaze. And as he leaned back from Terri, his mouth moving as he spoke in low tones that Keelin couldn't hear, she used the time she had before he would come to talk to her as best she could. To force strength into her spine, to take control of her emotions and damp them down so that she could talk to him without wavering or giving herself away.

Terri disappeared into the house with a final backward glance, a sad smile and a wave of her hand; Garrett then walked down the path, his eyes fixed on Keelin's face until he stopped a couple of feet from where she stood waiting.

'Thank you for bringing her home.'

'No problem.'

She couldn't keep looking at him. No matter how much she wanted to prove that she could without faltering or reaching out for him, she just couldn't do it. It hurt too much. So she turned her face away and took a moment to purse her lips together as she fought for control.

Garrett stepped closer. 'I didn't realize just how attached she had gotten to you so fast.'

Keelin laughed a little nervously, risking a glance at his broad chest from the corner of her eye. 'Well, despite what anyone else thinks there's apparently no time restriction on learning to care about someone.'

He stopped.

And Keelin closed her eyes for a brief second as she realized what she had just said and how it could be interpreted. So she tried to hide it behind an accusation instead. 'Though maybe if you hadn't forbidden her from ever talking to me again it mightn't have made it all the more important to her. You have a thing or two to learn about reverse psychology.'

'If I'd have known how important it already was to her then I would never have forbidden her to talk to you or write to you. I just thought it was easier for her to let go of any notion she had of you being a permanent fixture before she had the idea so firm in her mind that it was already a reality to her. She may think she's grown up Keelin, but she's not;

she's still a kid. And kids get hurt easily when someone leaves them.'

Despite the soft tone to his voice, Keelin glared up at him, her voice shaking almost as much as her body was. 'And it had nothing at all to do with how *you* felt about me, did it, Garrett? If you think for one second that I care so little about Terri that I wouldn't be a friend to her if she asked me to then you really don't have the faintest idea of the kind of person I am. And maybe I should have listened at the start when you warned me off befriending her, but you didn't do the same thing with her, did you? And now that she wants me to be at the other end of a phone from her I always will be. *Always.*'

She turned around, angrily swinging the gate open so hard that it rattled off the fence-line before she marched towards her car. The further away from him, the better.

Her hand was on the car door when his voice sounded behind her. 'All right. Maybe it had more to do with how I feel about you than it did with trusting you'd be there for her. And I won't try and stop her from talking to you, Keelin. You're there for her when she needs a listening ear on subjects she obviously can't talk to me about. And even though I really hate that, I'm glad that she has you.'

Keelin scowled down at the door handle. 'I would never do anything to come between you. She just needs a woman to talk to from time to time. That's all.'

'What she really needs is a mother. But I can't force someone to be that to her. That's not the kind of relationship you can make happen. I guess a friend like you is the next best thing.'

'I love her, Garrett. And maybe I have no business feeling that way in such a short amount of time, but it's there, and I don't want it gone. I've felt that way about your family almost from the first night. Maybe that's just a sign of how desperately I want that kind of a family for myself one day. But it's how I feel now—' she risked a glance at him from the corner of her eye '—and you can't force me to feel any differently.'

Garrett was in front of her car, like some kind of human roadblock, his dark brows creased into a frown as he stared at her. A muscle worked in his jaw as he looked towards the house, then back. His chest rose and fell as he took several long breaths. But he remained silent.

So Keelin yanked the car door open.

'*Wait.*'

She froze.

And her heart was thundering so loudly in her ears that she almost didn't hear the softly spoken plea.

'Don't go.'

CHAPTER FIFTEEN

KEELIN wasn't sure she had heard what Garrett had said correctly. So she turned her face in his direction, her wide eyes searching his for some kind of confirmation that he *had* said it. She couldn't take a chance on her traitorous heart having convinced her mind that he'd said it just because she wanted so badly for him to say it.

Garrett meanwhile was still frowning, his thick lashes flickering slightly as he looked down at the shining bonnet of her car and then back up into her eyes.

Then he said it more firmly. 'Don't go.'

Keelin shook her head, her voice breathless. 'You don't want me here.'

'You're wrong about that. I want you here more than I could ever begin to tell you.'

'But you didn't even want Terri to ever speak to me again!'

'And you were right—some of that *was* because of the way I felt about you. I didn't think I would cope too well having to hear her talk about you all the time, or having the right to see you when I didn't.'

Keelin couldn't believe he was saying these things to her. And she was finding it increasingly difficult to breathe. 'I didn't think you wanted the right to see me again. Not after the last time we spoke.'

He grimaced. 'I should never have said the things I said to you then. But this isn't an easy thing for me, Keelin. Nothing about the way I've felt since I met you has made any sense. And while I was so busy fighting how I felt, I guess it was just easier to lash out at you than it was to discuss it with you.'

'And what is it that you think you feel?'

As if it was a sign of relief that she had asked him in such a soft tone, opening the door for him to make a full confession, he took a deep breath. His frown was replaced with a look of determination as he walked to her, gently removing her hand from the door before he closed it with the palm of his other hand. And then he used both hands to turn her shoulders, pushing her back a little until she was resting against the side of the car.

Then he let go, his body inches from hers as his multi-toned deep voice began to sound in a low, seductive half-whisper.

'I never believed that something this big could happen this fast. I thought it was something that had to have a firm foundation first: a friendship, a common bond, shared interests. Hell, I don't know—*something*. It wasn't supposed to be something that was just there without any invitation or warning sign that it was coming. So, I fought it. I tried very hard to convince myself it wasn't real. But it's real, Keelin. And if I didn't know that from how much it hurt when you left last time, then I'd have known it from how I felt when I saw you again today.'

Keelin still couldn't speak.

And Garrett studied her face for a very long time before he smiled at her. 'I thought I would make a fool of myself if I asked you to stay. But Dermot very kindly pointed out to me that I was more of a fool for *not* asking. We had quite a debate about it, as it happens. You see, he still believes to this day that if he'd

fought to keep your mother then things might have been different. And he didn't want me to make the same mistake he had.'

Was that what Dermot had meant when he had talked about
it being sad if history were to repeat itself? Keelin had been so
sure that he was trying to make sure she wouldn't hurt Garrett
unintentionally. When maybe what he had been trying to say was
that she shouldn't be afraid to take a chance on what was there?

She swallowed hard. 'He was right, I think. I finished
reading the letters. And it wasn't that she ever stopped loving
him. In fact I think that's maybe why she never married. She
left here to continue her career when she was offered an art
bursary and when Dermot didn't talk to her about coming back
they just kind of drifted away from each other. And neither of
them ever had the courage to try and fight for what they had.
It's very sad. It could have been so very different for them. But
he had your mother, and he had you, and my mother had this
amazingly glittering career and me, so they weren't alone.'

'No, they weren't.'

With more hope in her heart than she had felt since she
could remember, Keelin reached out and took Garrett's hand
in hers, tangling their fingers and squeezing hard before she
spoke again. 'But I don't want that to happen to us.'

His other hand rose and framed the side of her face, fingers
threading into her hair as they had the night he had kissed her.
'Then don't go this time, Keelin. Stay and let me persuade you
to love me as much as I already love you. If we make the time
to build a better foundation, then we can find a way of making
this work.'

She opened her mouth to tell him what was already there
in her heart.

But he kept talking. As if he was very sure he had to persuade
her more before she would stay. 'I know you have responsibilities away from here, and I know that making the adjust-

ment to live in a place like this wouldn't be easy. But something as special as this is worth finding a compromise for, don't you think? So long as we knew it was what we both wanted we'd find a way around everything else. And you already love my family, and they love you. So stay. And I promise I won't try to push you away any more.'

Was it any wonder she had fallen so hard so fast for this man? All of this had been there the whole time, beneath the surface, waiting for him to find the right person to trust it to. And Keelin felt deeply humbled that he had chosen her. That, despite how much they had both fought against the inevitable, he had found the courage to tell her the truth and take a chance when the last time he had laid it on the line the woman in question had rejected him and walked away.

But that wasn't happening this time.

'You can't persuade someone to love you, Garrett—'

'I can make a damn good try. I'm not normally as much of a bastard as I've been with you this last while.'

She laughed at his words. 'I wasn't exactly sugar and spice myself. But you don't have to do any persuading, really you don't. I've been in love with you since you walked out of the mist that very first day.'

His beautiful toffee eyes widened in surprise. 'You have?'

Keelin nodded firmly. 'Yes, I have. But if it makes you feel any better I fought it every step of the way as well. I don't believe in love at first sight.'

'Neither do I.'

They both laughed at the same time. Then Keelin wrapped her free arm around his waist and pulled him closer, so that she was sandwiched between the cold metal of the car and the heat of his body.

She tilted her chin, her eyes shimmering as she smiled up at him. 'And yet here we are.'

Garrett smiled down at her with a full-blown, dimpled smile and so much open love in his eyes that Keelin could have died from joyful happiness there and then.

'So, you'll stay and we'll give this a go?'

'No.' When his smile faded she bundled the hand on his back into a fist full of shirt and tugged hard. 'I'll stay and we'll *fight* every day to make this work. Because I think that's what two people are supposed to do. And maybe we don't have to have the foundations we both thought we had to, to begin with. Maybe for us that will all build along the way. Maybe our foundation *is* the love that's already there. It's our gift. And how we use it to build everything else on is up to us.'

His head lowered towards hers, his voice a low grumble. 'How did you get to be so wise a woman?'

She tilted her head and grinned at him. 'I found what was missing in my life, where I truly belong. Things just have a tendency to get a little clearer when that happens.'

'You know I'm going to marry you.'

'Yes, you are.'

'But we'll wait a while and sort everything else out first so that there are no stumbling blocks along the way. And then I'll make a proper job of asking you. I want our marriage to work right from the start.'

Keelin nodded again. 'I agree. We should try and be practical, too, to set an example to our children if nothing else. If they all run off and get married inside a couple of weeks of meeting someone they'll take years off both our lives.'

The long fingers in her hair that had been absent-mindedly caressing the back of her head stilled, his other hand squeezing her fingers tightly. 'Do you want children with me, Keelin?'

'Yes.' The word came out on a sigh. 'Yes, I want that very much. I want a house *full* of them. I want Terri to have a ton of brothers and sisters who look just like her. You're a great father,

Garrett; even when you do get it wrong from time to time, you still keep trying to do what you think is best. How could I not want my children to have a father like that?'

Garrett went very still against her, only the rapid rise and fall of his chest against her breasts indicating how much her words had meant to him. Until he lowered his head again, his mouth hovering over hers as he stared into her eyes.

'You really have no idea how much I love you.'

Keelin smiled as she whispered back. 'Having now discussed the entire rest of our lives inside a week and a bit of first meeting each other, maybe it would just be better if you showed me?'

'Now, that I can do.'

Leaning the hard length of his body even tighter against hers, he brushed his mouth over hers, his eyes still open. Almost as if, were he to take a chance and close them, she might disappear before his eyes. And Keelin understood that, because she had dreamed this dream so many times since she'd left Valentia Island. When she closed her eyes the happily ever after would be there, until something would awaken her, and when she opened them she always found herself alone again.

But not this time. *Never again.* This was as real as it got and better than any dream she could ever have had.

She untangled her fingers from his so that she could wrap her arms around his neck to draw him into a deeper kiss. While she felt the deep groan in his chest rumbling through to tingle against her breasts and as she watched his eyes finally flutter closed in surrender to the moment, Keelin knew that they had the happily ever after to go with Garrett's happily-ever-after house. They were going to work hard to build the life that her mother and Dermot had missed out on together.

Somehow Keelin knew that her mother would be smiling down on them. Because she had brought her daughter to this tiny place off the coast of Kerry, hadn't she? She had placed her there in a painting decades before, as if she had somehow known that this was the place where she was meant to be.

And as far as her daughter was concerned, people who didn't believe in things like fate and love at first sight could just sit back and watch while Keelin and Garrett proved them wrong.

EPILOGUE

'WELL, if everyone thought we were insane to be in love after a few days they're going to have a field-day with this, aren't they?'

'The joys of living in a small community, my love. You'll get used to wagging tongues after a decade or so. It comes with the territory.'

'They're all waiting for us to fail, though, aren't they?' She smiled up at him.

And he nodded with an accompanying answering smile. 'Some of them probably are. As people get older they think that nothing this romantic could ever happen in real life, and *last*.'

'Ah, but we're proving them wrong. *The cynics*.'

'Yes, we are.' He drew her into his arms and together they looked out over the wide expanse of ocean and sky. It was a perfect day, the Atlantic reflecting the pale blue sky above while the gentle rhythm of waves hit the cliffs below.

And Keelin sighed in contentment. Yes, they would probably have the odd glitch thrown at them by life along the way, some glitches bigger then others, but she had complete faith that they would get through them as long as they were together.

They had more than just love as a foundation now. They had fought side by side to find a way of making things work for them, combining the elements of their lives that had once been a large part of their reasons for not allowing themselves to believe what they had could ever last.

Now they were moving into the house that Garrett had built before they'd ever met. Their happily-ever-after house as Keelin called it, which was a source of great amusement to both Garrett and Terri. But she could cope with their teasing, with the way they would quite often join forces to make her laugh with their back-and-forth bantering.

Yes, the very odd time, she would still disagree with Garrett, and they would debate at length, sometimes heatedly. But they both knew that the disagreements would ultimately end in compromise and some lengthy 'making up'. And no matter how angry or frustrated they might get in a single moment, it in no way could diminish from the depth of emotion they felt for each other.

That was why she knew the cynics could say what they liked. Time would prove them wrong. And she would smile sweetly at everyone who ever doubted them when she was old and grey and still had Garrett by her side.

He tilted his chin to look down at her face. 'You ready to go back yet?'

She smiled. 'No, just a minute more.'

Garrett chuckled. 'All right. One minute. But the sooner we go back, the sooner we can get away.'

'You have a point there.'

He settled his chin against her forehead again and breathed deeply, inhaling the familiar scent of her perfume mixed with the scent of the ocean and fresh air. And he honestly couldn't remember a time when he'd felt more at peace.

It was like the calm after the last of the island's winter storms. All the time that he had spent wrestling with his emotions and not daring to trust that something as right as this could be real for him were gone. And instead he had learned to talk everything through with her, even when they didn't agree, to trust in the fact that he was a stronger man for the fact that he had Keelin by his side.

What had once seemed so irrational to him now made perfect sense. They fitted. They were meant to be.

And, together with Terri and Dermot, they were a strong family unit. The Kincaids against the world.

'Dad! You have to bring Keelin back now,' Terri's voice yelled across at them from the open marquee set up with the lighthouse as a backdrop. 'Gramps says if he doesn't get to do his speech soon he'll have had too much champagne to speak.'

Keelin laughed.

And Garrett released her to allow her to gather up the long skirts of her white dress. 'Don't laugh. He's probably right. He was more nervous this morning than I was so I think he's been downing champagne in relief that nothing went wrong.'

One elegantly arched brow quirked at him in disbelief as she made her way across the grass by his side. 'You said you weren't nervous.'

He shrugged. 'I wasn't. I knew that marrying you was the most right thing I've ever done, so all that mattered to me was doing it. It was Dermot who was determined it should be the event of the island's history.'

'It was beautiful, though.'

And it had been. The moment she had walked down the narrow aisle of the tiny island chapel on Dermot's arm had been the moment that Garrett had thought he would die from happiness.

'Yes, it was.' He stood in front of her and pressed a firm, warm kiss to her mouth before whispering. 'But not as beautiful as you are, Mrs Kincaid.'

She sighed against his lips. 'Say it again.'

'I love you—' he kissed her again '—*Mrs Kincaid.*'

'*Da-ad!* Come on!'

Inside the marquee, her hand still firmly in his, Keelin looked around at the island's inhabitants and smiled. Then, just before Dermot tapped a glass for silence, she leaned up on tiptoe to whisper in her husband's ear.

'You know. We could have a baby straight away and arrange to have it born early. Then they would all think we got married inside six weeks because we had to. It might stop some of them from getting a headache trying to figure it out.'

Garrett laughed, leaning down to whisper his reply in his wife's ear. 'Well, first babies have a tendency to be late. But I'm willing to try if you are.'

Dermot dramatically cleared his throat as the room went silent. 'I'd just like to thank you all for coming at such short notice. And you all know I'm not a man of many words. But before they cut this lovely cake that they made down at Patrick's hotel in Knightstown—' there was a ripple of applause '—I'd just like a chance to welcome Keelin into the family.'

Keelin smiled across at him as the tears welled in her eyes.

'It was the proudest moment of my life to walk you up the aisle today, child. I know you and Garrett will be very happy and I'm glad that fate brought you here.' He cleared his throat as his voice crackled. 'You're the daughter I would always have wished for.'

Blinking through her tears as his voice broke and he had to swipe a tear from the corner of his eye, she mouthed a silent 'Thank you' across at him.

Her new father smiled in return and raised his glass high. 'The bride and groom!'

'*The bride and groom!*'

Keelin looked up at Garrett to find a shimmer in his eyes too and she had never loved him more. Then he lifted his hands to her face and brushed the tears from her cheeks with tender fingers before he leaned in to kiss her and whisper. 'Now you have your family, my love.'

'Yes, I do.'

And it *was* everything she could ever have wished for.

* * * * *

Every Life Has More
Than One Chapter™

Award-winning author Stevi Mittman delivers another
hysterical mystery, featuring Teddi Bayer, an irrepress-
ible heroine, and her to-die-for hero, Detective Drew
Scoones. After all, life on Long Island can be murder!

*Turn the page for a sneak peek
at the warm and funny fourth book,
WHOSE NUMBER IS UP, ANYWAY?,
in the Teddi Bayer series,
by STEVI MITTMAN.
On sale August 7*

CHAPTER 1

"Before redecorating a room, I always advise my clients to empty it of everything but one chair. Then I suggest they move that chair from place to place, sitting in it, until the placement feels right. Trust your instincts when deciding on furniture placement. Your room should "feel right.""

—TipsFromTeddi.com

Gut feelings. You know, that gnawing in the pit of your stomach that warns you that you are about to do the absolute stupidest thing you could do? Something that will ruin life as you know it?

I've got one now, standing at the butcher counter in King Kullen, the grocery store in the same strip mall as L.I. Lanes, the bowling alley cum billiard parlor I'm in the process of re-decorating for its "Grand Opening."

I realize being in the wrong supermarket probably doesn't sound exactly dire to you, but you aren't the one buying your father a brisket at a store your mother will somehow know isn't Waldbaum's.

And then, June Bayer isn't your mother.

The woman behind the counter has agreed to go into the freezer to find a brisket for me, since there aren't any in the case. There are packages of pork tenderloin, piles of spare ribs and rolls of sausage, but no briskets.

Warning Number Two, right? I should be so out of here.

But no, I'm still in the same spot when she comes back out, brisketless, her face ashen. She opens her mouth as if she is going to scream, but only a gurgle comes out.

And then she pinballs out from behind the counter, knocking bottles of Peter Luger Steak Sauce to the floor on her way, now hitting the tower of cans at the end of the prepared foods aisle and sending them sprawling, now making her way down the aisle, careening from side to side as she goes.

Finally, from a distance, I hear her shout, "He's deeeeeeaaaad! Joey's deeeeeaaaad."

My first thought is *You should always trust your gut.*

My second thought is that now, somehow, my mother will know I was in King Kullen. For weeks I will have to hear "What did you expect?" as though whenever you go to King Kullen someone turns up dead. And if the detective investigating the case turns out to be Detective Drew Scoones…well, I'll never hear the end of that from her, either.

She still suspects I murdered the guy who was found dead on my doorstep last Halloween just to get Drew back into my life.

Several people head for the butcher's freezer and I position myself to block them. If there's one thing I've learned from finding people dead—and the guy on my doorstep wasn't the first one—it's that the police get very testy when you mess with their murder scenes.

"You can't go in there until the police get here," I say, stationing myself at the end of the butcher's counter and in front of the Employees Only door, acting as if I'm some sort of authority. "You'll contaminate the evidence if it turns out to be murder."

Shouts and chaos. You'd think I'd know better than to throw

the word *murder* around. Cell phones are flipping open and tongues are wagging.

I amend my statement quickly. "Which, of course, it probably isn't. Murder, I mean. People die all the time, and it's not always in hospitals or their own beds, or…" I babble when I'm nervous, and the idea of someone dead on the other side of the freezer door makes me very nervous.

So does the idea of seeing Drew Scoones again. Drew and I have this on-again, off-again sort of thing…that I kind of turned off.

Who knew he'd take it so personally when he tried to get serious and I responded by saying we could talk about *us* tomorrow—and then caught a plane to my parents' condo in Boca the next day? In July. In the middle of a job.

For some crazy reason, he took that to mean that I was avoiding him and the subject of *us*.

That was three months ago. I haven't seen him since.

The manager, who identifies himself and points to his name-plate in case I don't believe him, says he has to go into *his cooler.* "Maybe Joey's not dead," he says. "Maybe he can be saved, and you're letting him die in there. Did you ever think of that?"

In fact, I hadn't. But I had thought that the murderer might try to go back in to make sure his tracks were covered, so I say that I will go in and check.

Which means that the manager and I couple up and go in together while everyone pushes against the doorway to peer in, erasing any chance of finding clean prints on that Employee Only door.

I expect to find carcasses of dead animals hanging from hooks, and maybe Joey hanging from one, too. I think it's going to be very creepy and I steel myself, only to find a rather benign series of shelves with large slabs of meat laid out carefully on them, along with boxes and boxes marked simply Chicken.

Nothing scary here, unless you count the body of a middle-aged man with graying hair sprawled faceup on the floor. His eyes are wide open and unblinking. His shirt is stiff. His pants are stiff. His body is stiff. And his expression, you should forgive the pun—is frozen. Bill-the-manager crosses himself and stands mute while I pronounce the guy dead in a sort of *happy now?* tone.

"We should not be in here," I say, and he nods his head emphatically and helps me push people out of the doorway just in time to hear the police sirens and see the cop cars pull up outside the big store windows.

Bobbie Lyons, my partner in Teddi Bayer Interior Designs (and also my neighbor, my best friend and my private fashion police), and Mark, our carpenter (and my dogsitter, confidant, and ego booster), rush in from next door. They beat the cops by a half step and shout out my name. People point in my direction.

After all the publicity that followed the unfortunate incident during which I shot my ex-husband, Rio Gallo, and then the subsequent murder of my first client—which I solved, I might add—it seems like the whole world, or at least all of Long Island, knows who I am.

Mark asks if I'm all right. (Did I remember to mention that the man is drop-dead-gorgeous-but-a-decade-too-young-for-me-yet-too-old-for-my-daughter-thank-god?) I don't get a chance to answer him because the police are quickly closing in on the store manager and me.

"The woman—" I begin telling the police. Then I have to pause for the manager to fill in her name, which he does: *Fran.*

I continue. "Right. Fran. Fran went into the freezer to get a brisket. A moment later she came out and screamed that Joey was dead. So I'd say she was the one who discovered the body."

"And you are…?" the cop asks me. It comes out a bit like who do I *think* I am, rather than who am I really?

"An innocent bystander," Bobbie, hair perfect, makeup just right, says, carefully placing her body between the cop and me.

"And she was just leaving," Mark adds. They each take one of my arms.

Fran comes into the inner circle surrounding the cops. In case it isn't obvious from the hairnet and bloodstained white apron with Fran embroidered on it, I explain that she was the butcher who was going for the brisket. Mark and Bobbie take that as a signal that I've done my job and they can now get me out of there. They twist around, with me in the middle, as if we're a Rockettes line, until we are facing away from the butcher counter. They've managed to propel me a few steps toward the exit when disaster—in the form of a Mazda RX7 pulling up at the loading curb—strikes.

Mark's grip on my arm tightens like a vise. "Too late," he says.

Bobbie's expletive is unprintable. "Maybe there's a back door," she suggests, but Mark is right. It's too late.

I've laid my eyes on Detective Scoones. And while my gut is trying to warn me that my heart shouldn't go there, regions farther south are melting at just the sight of him.

"Walk," Bobbie orders me.

And I try to. Really.

Walk, I tell my feet. *Just put one foot in front of the other.*

I can do this because I know, in my heart of hearts, that if Drew Scoones was still interested in me, he'd have gotten in touch with me after I returned from Boca. And he didn't.

Since he's a detective, Drew doesn't have to wear one of those dark blue Nassau County Police uniforms. Instead, he's got on jeans, a tight-fitting T-shirt and a tweedy sports jacket. If you think that sounds good, you should see him. Chiseled features, cleft chin, brown hair that's naturally a little sandy in the front, a smile that…well, that doesn't matter. He isn't smiling now.

He walks up to me, tucks his sunglasses into his breast pocket and looks me over from head to toe.

"Well, if it isn't Miss Cut and Run," he says. "Aren't you supposed to be somewhere in Florida or something?" He looks at Mark accusingly, as if he was covering for me when he told Drew I was gone.

"Detective Scoones?" one of the uniforms says. "The stiff's in the cooler and the woman who found him is over there." He jerks his head in Fran's direction.

Drew continues to stare at me.

You know how when you were young, your mother always told you to wear clean underwear in case you were in an accident? And how, a little farther on, she told you not to go out in hair rollers because you never knew who you might see—or who might see you? And how now your best friend says she wouldn't be caught dead without makeup and suggests you shouldn't either?

Okay, today, *finally,* in my overalls and Converse sneakers, I get it.

I brush my hair out of my eyes. "Well, I'm back," I say. As if he hasn't known my exact whereabouts. The man is a detective, for heaven's sake. "Been back awhile."

Bobbie has watched the exchange and apparently decided she's given Drew all the time he deserves. "And we've got work to do, so…" she says, grabbing my arm and giving Drew a little two-fingered wave goodbye.

As I back up a foot or two, the store manager sees his chance and places himself in front of Drew, trying to get his attention. Maybe what makes Drew such a good detective is his ability to focus.

Only what he's focusing on is me.

"Phone broken? Carrier pigeon died?" he asks me, taking in Fran, the manager, the meat counter and that Employees Only door, all without taking his eyes off me.

Mark tries to break the spell. "We've got work to do there,

you've got work to do here, Scoones," Mark says to him, gesturing toward next door. "So it's back to the alley for us."

Drew's lip twitches. "You working the alley now?" he says.

"If you'd like to follow me," Bill-the-manager, clearly exasperated, says to Drew—who doesn't respond. It's as if waiting for my answer is all he has to do.

So, fine. "You knew I was back," I say.

The man has known my whereabouts every hour of the day for as long as I've known him. And my mother's not the only one who won't buy that he "just happened" to answer this particular call. In fact, I'm willing to bet my children's lunch money that he's taken every call within ten miles of my home since the day I got back.

And now he's gotten lucky.

"*You* could have called *me*," I say.

"You're the one who said *tomorrow* for our talk and then flew the coop, chickie," he says. "I figured the ball was in your court."

"Detective?" the uniform says. "There's something you ought to see in here."

Drew gives me a look that amounts to *in or out?*

He could be talking about the investigation, or about our relationship.

Bobbie tries to steer me away. Mark's fists are balled. Drew waits me out, knowing I won't be able to resist what might be a murder investigation.

Finally he turns and heads for the cooler.

And, like a puppy dog, I follow.

Bobbie grabs the back of my shirt and pulls me to a halt.

"I'm just going to show him something," I say, yanking away.

"Yeah," Bobbie says, pointedly looking at the buttons on my blouse. The two at breast level have popped. "That's what I'm afraid of."

HARLEQUIN®

Super Romance®

*Looking for a romantic, emotional
and unforgettable escape?*

*You'll find it this month and every month
with a Harlequin Superromance!*

Rory Gorenzi has a sense of humor and a sense of
honor. She also happens to be good with children.

Seamus Lee, widower and father of four, needs
someone with exactly those traits.

They meet at the Colorado mountain school owned
by Rory's father, where she teaches skiing and
avalanche safety. But Seamus—and his children—
learn more from her than that....

Look for

GOOD WITH CHILDREN

by Margot Early,

*available August 2007, and these other
fantastic titles from Harlequin Superromance.*

REASONS FOR REVENGE

A brand-new provocative miniseries by *USA TODAY*
bestselling author **Maureen Child** begins with

SCORNED
BY THE BOSS

Jefferson Lyon is a man used to having his own way.
He runs his shipping empire from California, and
his admin Caitlyn Monroe runs the rest of his world.
When Caitlin decides she's had enough and needs
new scenery, Jefferson devises a plan to get her back.
Jefferson *never* loses, but little does he know that
he's in a competition....

Don't miss any of the other titles from the
REASONS FOR REVENGE trilogy by
USA TODAY bestselling author **Maureen Child**.

SCORNED BY THE BOSS #1816
Available August 2007

SEDUCED BY THE RICH MAN #1820
Available September 2007

CAPTURED BY THE BILLIONAIRE #1826
Available October 2007

Only from Silhouette Desire!

REQUEST YOUR FREE BOOKS!
2 FREE NOVELS PLUS 2
FREE GIFTS!

HARLEQUIN ROMANCE®

From the Heart, For the Heart

YES! Please send me 2 FREE Harlequin Romance® novels and my 2 FREE gifts. After receiving them, if I don't wish to receive any more books, I can return the shipping statement marked "cancel." If I don't cancel, I will receive 4 brand-new novels every month and be billed just $3.57 per book in the U.S., or $4.05 per book in Canada, plus 25¢ shipping and handling per book and applicable taxes, if any*. That's a savings of over 15% off the cover price! I understand that accepting the 2 free books and gifts places me under no obligation to buy anything. I can always return a shipment and cancel at any time. Even if I never buy another book from Harlequin, the two free books and gifts are mine to keep forever.

114 HDN EEV7 314 HDN EEWK

Name _____ (PLEASE PRINT) _____

Address _____ Apt. _____

City _____ State/Prov. _____ Zip/Postal Code _____

Signature (if under 18, a parent or guardian must sign)

Mail to the **Harlequin Reader Service®:**
IN U.S.A.: P.O. Box 1867, Buffalo, NY 14240-1867
IN CANADA: P.O. Box 609, Fort Erie, Ontario L2A 5X3

Not valid to current Harlequin Romance subscribers.

Want to try two free books from another line?
Call 1-800-873-8635 or visit www.morefreebooks.com.

* Terms and prices subject to change without notice. NY residents add applicable sales tax. Canadian residents will be charged applicable provincial taxes and GST. This offer is limited to one order per household. All orders subject to approval. Credit or debit balances in a customer's account(s) may be offset by any other outstanding balance owed by or to the customer. Please allow 4 to 6 weeks for delivery.

Your Privacy: Harlequin is committed to protecting your privacy. Our Privacy Policy is available online at www.eHarlequin.com or upon request from the Reader Service. From time to time we make our lists of customers available to reputable firms who may have a product or service of interest to you. If you would prefer we not share your name and address, please check here. ☐

HR07

Coming Next Month

#3967 MARRYING HER BILLIONAIRE BOSS Myrna Mackenzie
Black sheep Carson Banick needs a wife to save his family's fortune.
Beth Crayton, Carson's feisty PA, is determined to succeed on her own,
without a man. As the attraction between them grows, Carson must decide
what's more important: saving his family, or claiming Beth's heart?

#3968 THE ITALIAN'S WIFE BY SUNSET Lucy Gordon
The Rinucci Brothers
Sensible Della Hadley should have known better than to embark on an affair
with irresistible playboy Carlo Rinucci. She knows such passion cannot last,
despite Carlo's protests that their love is forever. Can Carlo make Della his
bride before the sun sets on their affair?

#3969 HIS MIRACLE BRIDE Marion Lennox
Castle at Dolphin Bay
Shanni Jefferson doesn't do family! But when she finds herself a live-in
nanny to five little children—and working side by side with their gorgeous
guardian Pierce MacLaughlin—she begins to wonder whether family life with
this adorable brood might suit her after all.

#3970 REUNITED: MARRIAGE IN A MILLION Liz Fielding
Secrets We Keep
Popular TV presenter Belle is married to gorgeous billionaire Ivo, and lives in
a beautiful mansion. Yet beneath the veneer of her perfect life is the truth of
their marriage of convenience. But Belle is deeply in love with Ivo, and only
wishes for a baby to make their family whole.

#3971 BABY TWINS: PARENTS NEEDED Teresa Carpenter
Baby on Board
Rachel Adams's independent life is turned upside down when she's named
guardian to two orphaned twins! Then gorgeous co-guardian Ford Sullivan
turns up. Being this close to Ford makes Rachel wonder whether stand-in
mom and dad could become forever bride and groom?

#3972 BREAK UP TO MAKE UP Fiona Harper
Nick and Adele Hughes's marriage is over. But, stranded in a picturesque
cottage, they find they cannot resist the spark that has always fizzed
between them. As the twinkling firelight works its magic, Nick and Adele
discover that the wonderful thing about breaking up is making up.

HRCNM0707